FADING FAME

Women of a Certain Age in Hollywood

Congratulations,
Renee!
Hope you enjoy the book —
Pam Munter

Fading Fame

Women of a Certain Age in Hollywood

ten short stories & two short plays

by

PAM MUNTER

BOOKS

Adelaide Books
New York / Lisbon
2021

FADING FAME
Women of a Certain Age in Hollywood

ten short stories & two short plays
By Pam Munter

Published by Adelaide Books, New York / Lisbon
adelaidebooks.org

Editor-in-Chief
Stevan V. Nikolic

For any information, please address Adelaide Books
at info@adelaidebooks.org
or write to:
Adelaide Books
244 Fifth Ave. Suite D27
New York, NY, 10001

ISBN: 978-1-954351-76-9
Printed in the United States of America

Contents

"Fame, if you win it,
Comes and goes in a minute.
Where's the real stuff in life to cling to?"

(from "Make Someone Happy," music by Jule Stein, lyrics by
Betty Comden and Adolph Green, ©1960 by Stratford Music Corp;
Chappell & Co, Administrator)

Foreword

The Hollywood of the 1950s was a mysterious, magical place. It was long before VCRs, digital replays, the *National Enquirer* or the 24-hour news cycle. The only way one could watch a movie was in the theater and all we knew about movie stars came from the studios that controlled the information flow. Those all-powerful monoliths manufactured and synthesized stories and fed them to movie magazines, transforming mere fiction into mythology. The only way we knew when someone married or divorced was when legal documents became public. We didn't know who was chemically dependent, a spousal abuser, or a child molester.

Still, there was one deviant behavior we all assumed was going on. The casting couch was a persistent legend all its own. The way to the top for actresses was through the back offices of power brokers Darryl F. Zanuck, Louis B. Mayer, David O. Selznick, Harry Cohn and even the elderly Adolph Zukor.

We didn't think it particularly shocking because women were already about as far from a protected legal class as possible. We couldn't own property in our own name, adopt a child without a man, or be a party to a contract without a man's signature. Women's subservient nature was considered inherent in the species, a form of institutional discrimination. It was widely assumed that women comprised a secondary class whose main purpose was to serve the needs of men. We saw it in our own homes, and watched it powerfully modeled on the screen. Even with the fleeting promise of a feminist theme (think Katharine Hepburn or Rosalind Russell), the closing scene inevitably featured the woman caving to consensual male superiority.

The short stories in this collection demonstrate the costs of that institutional social oppression. As with all historical fiction, some of the people described here lived at one time, but the stories are fabricated via imagination. The "Hollywood" in the book's title serves as a metaphor for show business and is not restricted to the geography of Southern California. Misogyny and the struggle to maintain a sense of integrity in the performing arts are not unique to time and place.

Women were welcomed into show business with the subtext clear and inevitable. If you were young, beautiful, nubile and willing, you stood a chance at fame. Talent didn't hurt, but it wasn't required. The eventual deal-breaker was the aging process. As women grew older, they became less desirable as sex objects, on and off the screen, and were easily replaced by eager, younger, compliant models.

What happens to women whose fame fades? For many, the impassioned striving for stardom defined their very existence. The women in these stories did achieve a measure of it and all paid a price, some more than the rest.

The opening story, "Frances," takes place in the earliest days of Hollywood. It depicts the painful deterioration of "America's Sweetheart," Mary Pickford, a film icon and the first woman to run a motion picture studio. Sadly, it seems the real survivor in this story was her favorite Oscar-winning screenwriter, Frances Marion, wasn't under the same pressures to conform to the Hollywood mold. Still, she would get caught up in it, just like everyone else. Her biggest successes and two Academy Awards came when under contract to MGM. Pickford and Marion were friends for over thirty years, but our fictional version speculates that Marion might have wanted more.

In "Dinner with Daddy," Irene Mayer Selznick comes "home" to Bel Air for the first time in years after escaping the burden as the youngest daughter of MGM mogul Louis B. Mayer. She grew up surrounded by movie stars, but her commanding and controlling father thought he was protecting her by prohibiting her from going near his studio – or any of his actors. Instead, she defiantly married David O. Selznick, who ran a competing studio, but again became subservient to a dominant male. Her existential escape came when she produced the megahit on Broadway, "A Streetcar Named Desire." Of all the stories' faded heroines, perhaps only Irene was a true survivor. In this imagined tale, she confronts her tyrannical, abusive father and her past. Feminists may cringe, but will cheer her on.

"Delayed Flight" underscores the insularity and loneliness of the acting profession and the perpetual vulnerability felt by its female stars. To continue to be successful one must remain beautiful. Transformation is often internal, as well. What happens when an actress encounters her unresolved past in the form of her high school drama teacher on a plane?

"The Last Fan" stars Joan Davis, a television star from the 1950s, who enjoyed a long career in vaudeville and in movies. She invested well and lived comfortably to the end of her life in the climes of Palm Springs. But it didn't insulate her from the loneliness and neediness of an unfulfilled existence, made obvious after her TV series was canceled. When the striving is done, what happens to a woman's well-being? She sought companionship with another former star, Eddie Cantor, but he's famously married with five daughters. With stardom no longer possible, she longs for both affection and adulation until she seems to find it in "The Last Fan."

During her heyday, Doris Day never had much of a life outside her fame. The demands to perform started long before adolescence. She spent her life in the company of men, many of whom helped her forge one of the most successful and long-lived careers in movies, records, radio and television. The cost was not only the millions her third husband stole from her, but likely her identity as well. In "Deconstructing Doris," it's evident that she grew dependent on her son, the only available remaining male, for support once her husbands had disappeared.

What happens when a performer loses her audience? She moves down the venue food chain, from the big time to hotel conference rooms. In "The Curtain Never Falls," the protagonist is physically unable to keep up with her own reputation for high-energy performances and the adjustment proves to be challenging. Sometimes, however, fate has something else in mind. Fame might return in a totally unexpected way.

"Madelyn, Mostly" describes how engulfing and exhausting it can be to maintain a singing career, especially at "a certain age." It's challenging to create a personal life when you're always on the road, performing songs from the Great American Songbook to a new group of strangers every night. It's easy to become preoccupied with those lyrics that willfully invade and inundate the subconscious mind. The words can offer meaning, filling the void when one's internal house remains sparsely furnished. Like most performers here, she turned to a series of men for comfort, but they couldn't forestall the encroaching pathology.

"Everything That Mattered" tells the story of troubled, talented singer Susannah McCorkle who wanted fame almost more than anything. She, too, sought solace with a stream of men, often choosing them for their musical expertise and the professional doors they could open for her. Susannah struggled with more than misogyny, though. She had a depressive order; some say she was bipolar. This story takes place in New York City, but it could have happened anywhere.

"Ethel" was the most successful member of a multi-generational, royal theatrical family, already a star at 15. Now, nearing 75, she's at the close of a long career. No longer lighting up Broadway, she's a featured player in a Warner Bros. musical, playing the better part of herself opposite Frank Sinatra. Can she accept who she has become?

A supporting player with early onset dementia looks back on a long and varied career in "Gerry's Interview." A regular gig as a cowboy star's sidekick doesn't translate into economic stability when the series is canceled. Without irony, Gerry takes a job as a clerk at a movie studio, then leaps at the chance to answer fan mail for someone really famous. By the time she's rediscovered at nostalgia shows, it's almost too late. We track her rise and decline in her own unreliable words.

The plays may suggest more hope, or perhaps different solutions. If the short stories muck around the edges of tragedy, the plays may delight with a touch of dark comedy. "Life Without" is the story of a woman trying to cope with a singular kind of show biz-related loss. Starting her quest for fame too late, our protagonist reluctantly gave up her passion and has not been the same since. When she meets a man who might be able to get it back for her, she concocts a desperate way to get what she thinks she wants. But she finds herself preoccupied with old desires and almost loses an important relationship in the process.

"Janet Drake, Private Eye" tells of two women of a certain age, both having portrayed the same role at different times.

Now, each has a chance to restore their fame on the big screen. What will they give up in order to get it back?

The romanticized fiction that fame is a solution to everything is evident any place there is a stage and someone desperate to perform there. Some of these stories may use the names of real-life people but, rest assured, it's merely historical fiction. The women in this collection are past their prime, trying to find their way in a world that no longer finds them valuable. Who they were, they are no longer. Each one struggles within her own limitations, seeking to re-balance and create life anew, to find an option that could be described as Plan B. It's tempting to characterize these women as victims. In reality, they are strong, talented women doing the best they can in a toxic and often demeaning environment. We can't help but admire them. They are the fallout, the flotsam and jetsam, of a time when sexism was waved as proudly as a flag. The corrosive truth is that misogyny is not unique to Hollywood. Women of a certain age will all face these dilemmas. These are our sisters.

THE SHORT STORIES

Frances

The irony didn't escape Frances Marion that, although she was the premier screenwriter of her time, she couldn't find the right words to describe how she felt about Mary Pickford. Or why.

It didn't seem like that many years ago. World War I was raging but Hollywood was thriving, existing in a glittering cocoon. Frances had come to the editing room at Biograph and found Mary alone. She was startled when Mary turned around, her petite frame dominated by her big blue eyes and long, curly blonde hair. "I know we're going to be best friends," Mary had said within minutes of their meeting. "I don't have many friends," she had confided. "No time."

Frances knew it had to be more than that. Mary was an international icon, untouchable, unreachable some would say. The most powerful woman in the industry. That was more likely the issue. "I would like to be your friend," Frances echoed, carefully. An unfamiliar jolt came and went from within, like a blast of hot air. It wasn't at all unpleasant but surprised her with its intensity. Then again, she had never met a movie star before.

Now some 15 years later, Frances looked forward to seeing Mary again, even though she was unsure what she would find in that house tonight. There was a time when there was no ambivalence or anxiety about her dinners at Pickfair. They were fun, lively events full of lawn games, alcohol and opium. She found it odd that Hollywood's highest paid stars would find it hilarious to shoot home movies of each other, each trying to outdo the other with outrageousness. It was about making each other laugh and it wasn't hard to do. Someone would always be thrown into the huge pool in their evening clothes or go down the giant slide backwards.

That night, she had invited Bill, her fourth husband, to go with her. It had been a half-hearted gesture on her part.

"It'll just be another night of drinking," he said, his face stern.

"Since when has that bothered you?" She gestured to the wet bar that dominated the east wall of their spacious, well-appointed Hancock Park living room. So much unfinished business between them. All those times Bill would disappear into the night, returning a day or two later without explanation or apology. In spite of her best efforts, she had married another alcoholic. How had this happened again?

"You know what I mean. This whole town is drowning in booze."

He was right. Prohibition hadn't affected the community at all. And now that it was gone, the use of all chemicals, illegal and legal, ramped up right on schedule.

"You're not worried about driving in Beverly Hills, huh?"

"No. The studio is taking care of the ticket. They always do." She could trust the power of MGM's publicity honcho Howard Strickling to handle any difficulties with the law, no matter how severe. Even director Busby Berkeley's running down that poor, elderly woman on the sidewalk was finessed by the studio without any publicity. Frances wasn't worried about her own intake, anyway. That wasn't her poison. In fact, she would confront her much more forbidden addiction that very night.

"Why did she invite you, anyway? It's been years since you heard from her."

Frances knew that very well. She had missed her friend and dared to hope for a deeper connection, though so many years had passed. "I don't know. Maybe it was by mistake. But I'm going."

Bill returned to his magazine.

"What will you do while I'm gone?" she asked even though she knew his response would be a lie. His latest girlfriend was probably waiting down the block, watching for Frances to leave.

"Oh, I dunno. Probably just listen to the radio and look through magazines. I might go to bed early."

Looking over at his stooped frame, she wondered why she had married Bill after knowing him such a short time. He wasn't smart, their sex was a cruel joke and the more she thought about it, she didn't like him much personally, either. There must be a reason she had gone through four husbands, each impotent in his own way – perverse, inept, clumsy or drunk. She wasn't sure what it was but now and again, inklings of other possibilities caused her too much discomfort to pursue the thoughts any further.

It had been at least a decade since Frances had been invited to Pickfair, the iconic Beverly Hills home of silent movie stars Mary Pickford and Douglas Fairbanks. There hadn't been a falling out, not really, but the distance between Frances and Mary seemed to grow imperceptibly over the years. Hollywood itself had gone through cataclysmic transitions. Just five years ago, silent movies had abruptly given way to the talkies. Major studios had morphed into rapacious whales, gobbling up the smaller fish. Even Mary's United Artists had experienced pressure from the biggies. And poor little Mary. She was a casualty, too. She had quit the movies. Or did they quit her? Frances' screenwriting career had taken off and she was now the highest paid in the business, male or female.

Frances eased herself into her newly waxed, burgundy Auburn Phaeton convertible. It had taken most of her screenwriter's salary from "The Champ" to pay for it. For her, the car wasn't just a Hollywood status symbol, but a reflection of her conspicuous success in the industry. It made her feel almost invincible. She turned the key in the ignition and the roar of the engine revved her thoughts back to that first day, the morning she met Mary so many years earlier.

Frances was looking for a job as an artist, hoping to create portraits of Mary for movie posters. Instead, she was surprised and a little thrilled at how quickly their friendship had happened. They were almost combustible together—thoughts, ideas, shared experiences sparking the air almost from the start.

Frances drove down the darkened and nearly deserted Sunset Boulevard toward Pickfair, keeping an eye out for any motorcycle cops who might be watching for her car. For just an instant, she thought about returning home and ambushing Bill but thought better of it. It might be fun, she mused, but she really didn't care. This marriage, like the last, would be over soon. She would divorce him and move on, as she always did.

As she checked her lipstick in the mirror, she realized that it had been so long since they'd been in touch that Mary didn't know about the last two husbands. Well, Mary knew about the first one because they'd talked about their love lives over drinks one night at the Sunset Inn. The drinks just kept coming that night and before she knew it, Mary had told Frances about her hardscrabble childhood on the road while playing burlesque houses, something she never confessed to anyone. How she had been fondled and even raped by older men on the circuit. Maybe it was the highballs or perhaps being moved by the trust, but it made Frances cry. Mary got up from the table and walked around to comfort her, caressing her back ever so gently. When they stood up to leave, the long, tight hug elicited that same, now familiar tsunami, etched in her emotional memory bank and nurtured all these years. She was afraid to want more, wondering what it all meant. Still, after that evening, Frances was more careful about the extent of her alcohol intake around Mary.

The last time she saw Mary, she was still "America's Sweetheart," with her screen swashbuckler husband Douglas Fairbanks, ceremoniously placing their hands and feet in cement at Grauman's Chinese Theater. Flashbulbs popping and fans screaming, everyone wanting to touch Mary. Could that be five years ago already? Because of the size of the crowd and the reporters, Frances couldn't find a way to maneuver herself close to Mary. Even gossip maven Louella Parsons had trouble getting a quick interview for her radio show with the world-famous stars. After a while, Frances gave it up, settling for an enthusiastic wave to Mary from across the expansive forecourt.

In the rearview mirror, Frances saw the flashing red lights closing in on her car. Shit. She didn't think she had been going that much over the speed limit. She pulled over anyway, and cranked open the window.

"Oh, it's you, Miss Marion."

"Hello, officer. What can I do for you?"

"Have you been drinking?"

"Not yet."

"You were going mighty fast back there."

"I'm on my way to dinner with Mary Pickford and Douglas Fairbanks. Wouldn't you be in a hurry, too?"

He stared at her for a minute, probably not used to hearing those names as a defense for speeding. Frances remembered a conversation with Joan Crawford in the commissary a few days earlier. Joan had been stopped by this same Beverly Hills cop more than once and got out of the tickets by spending a few minutes with him in his back seat. She was getting a reputation, undoubtedly contributing to her rise at MGM. Frances hoped she wouldn't have to do that with this guy. She was coming to think of men as sexual marauders, anyway. Though she had made her mark in Hollywood without lying down, it wasn't because those studio bosses hadn't tried. She might have gone for Thalberg but he never came on to her, much to her disappointment. He had settled for that cross-eyed Norma Shearer. Tonight, her thoughts didn't linger on all that. Her mind and body were poised for the trip up the hill. She wasn't ready to admit to herself what she wanted from Mary, but it had nothing to do with this galoot cop.

"OK, Miss Marion. You be careful tonight."

"I will, officer."

She put the window back up, took a deep, relieved breath and continued up Beverly Drive to Summit. She was glad she hadn't reached for her flask along the way. There'd be plenty of booze once she arrived. Mary would see to that.

At the stop light, she resolved not to tell Mary about all the times she screened the silent movies they made together for her friends and her husbands. Or the times she watched them alone when Bill was out. Mary was never far away from her thoughts.

That day of their first meeting, Mary's physical presence and charisma were so riveting that Frances couldn't break her gaze. There was something in her manner that was vaguely seductive – the sideways glances, the sly smiles, the gentle touch on the shoulder. She dismissed it, knowing Mary was not only married but, back then, engaged in a secret and salacious affair with Douglas, whom she later married. She was glad Mary could confide in her about that. It had only brought them closer. Maybe Mary was, well, flirtatious with everyone, not just her. It was just her imagination. Even so. That feeling.

Frances often reassured herself that she wasn't "that way" and knew Mary wasn't, either. And yet, every once in a while, when they were together having drinks, Frances would have to fight off those thoughts, those intrusive and unwelcome pictures in her mind. Before they were vanquished, though, she took comfort in the certain knowledge Mary wouldn't be brutish or thoughtless and would always take her pleasure into account. Of course, Mary would have to make the first move. Frances was unwilling to linger on those daydreams. They made her nervous. It just wasn't right.

She turned right on Beverly Drive and headed up the hill. She had made that journey a hundred times, years ago. Tonight, she couldn't help but grin, remembering that wonderful day on the set when she and Mary had staged a revolution against the autocratic director, Maurice Tourneur. They'd become almost a single unit in moviemaking—Frances writing the screenplays and Mary in her customary starring role. In spite of their extraordinary success, they were both tired of the goody-two-shoes character Mary's public seemed to demand. One day on the set, she took Mary aside before the filming began.

"I think we need to have a little fun here, Sweetie. It's so stodgy. Same old stuff. We're shooting the hurricane scene today, right?"

Mary looked at her, eagerly awaiting her friend's idea and nodded. They had always loved laughing together.

"Now, when Frenchy says 'Roll 'em,' you trip over the furniture and…"

Mary joined in immediately. "…And then I'll bump into Hobart, knocking him over."

"Then," Frances said, "you are so surprised you fall backwards on to the couch and knock it over."

"I'll fall ungracefully to the floor then watch everyone's reaction." Mary leaned in closer to Frances to share the next part of the plot.

"And just when they think it's over, we'll have Hobart get up and pour a bucket of that hurricane on me."

They could hardly contain their anticipatory glee.

As soon as the camera was rolling, she pulled her prank. Frances watched behind the camera with her hands over her mouth as the cast and crew stifled gasps and laughter in equal amounts. This was not the self-contained, pure and innocent Mary they were used to seeing. The director was not at all amused. He bellowed out, "Cut! Cut! Cut! This is not in the script! You ladies are horrible. We need to get to work here. No more games, Miss Pickford, please."

By now everyone was cracking up and it took more than an hour to return to the serious business of making movies. With the towel wrapped over her dripping curls, Mary threw her arms around Frances in triumph. There was that electric jolt again.

Yes, they had been a team, all right.

She maneuvered her car up the long, winding driveway, the house lit up like one of Mary's movie sets. Even after all these years, she was impressed by the enormity of the house on the hill and the acres of surrounding grounds.

Hardly a day went by that Frances didn't think about her, wondering what she was doing and with whom. There had been a disagreement when Frances wasn't included by Mary in that big United Artists deal but that was so many years ago. And truthfully, Frances wasn't fond of Douglas from the start. He was a brash show-off, a little boy, she thought, and not nearly good enough for Mary. But then who was?

She already knew the answer to that, in spite of her best attempts to distract herself. It was a truth that had haunted her for many years, through four husbands and nearly twenty pictures with Mary.

She wondered why all this was skipping around in her brain tonight. What did she want to have happen tonight, anyway? Nothing, nothing, she reassured herself, grabbing the rim of the steering wheel more securely. Everything will be just fine. A lovely dinner with old friends, that's all. With the marriage winding down, maybe this would be the perfect time to reconnect with Mary. As a friend.

She left her car with a tall black valet and, stepping out into the night, felt enveloped by the sweet scent of jasmine. The oversized carved wooden door at the entrance swung open to reveal a formally dressed butler. She remembered him from all those years before. Morrison was his name. Yes, that was it. He must be close to seventy now. She admired how loyal Mary was to her employees, if not to her husbands.

"Come in please, Miss Marion. We're so happy you're here tonight. Miss Pickford has been looking forward to your arrival."

"Thank you, Morrison. I'm very glad to be here."

"Let me take your coat. It's chilly tonight, isn't it?"

It won't be for long, she thought.

"Congratulations on your Academy Award, Miss Marion. I enjoyed 'The Champ.' Very touching."

She smiled. She was used to such accolades. Even so, they made her feel special. Largely thanks to her work with Mary, she was admired as a brilliant screenwriter, a skill that would inevitably outlast beauty in the fickle Hollywood milieu.

"Thank you. That's very kind of you."

She stepped inside the ornately decorated foyer, full of cut flowers and Greek statuary. In the distance, she could hear the sounds of a string quartet.

Pickfair was just as she remembered it. It seemed that nothing had changed, right down to the intricate imported doilies on the arms of the couches. The rooms were still too commodious for human habitation, the overstuffed chairs almost comically dwarfing their guests. The living room, if it could be called that, could have accommodated a hundred or more people. There was nothing cozy or intimate about this place. She looked through the big windows toward the bright lights of the city in the distance, and it felt as if she had stepped into a time capsule some 15 years earlier. All the furniture was in the same places, an oversized ashtray dominating the center of each table, placed just so. Even the slipcovers looked to be the same pattern and color. She wondered what else had remained the same.

Frances scanned the room for Mary, not visible among the buzzing crowd. In fact, she had a hard time recognizing most of the 30 or so guests, milling about with drinks in hand. Off to her far left was the massive dining room, which she knew would be perfectly set. She hesitated for only a moment, then scooted unobtrusively down the long corridor. Scanning the room to the left and then to the right, she circled the massive dining room table, checking the place cards. There was an unfamiliar name to the right of Mary's card. She quickly found her own a few places down and switched the cards, giggling just a little. Mary would appreciate her sleight-of-hand and gesture of affection. Entering the living room again, Frances saw a young woman approach.

"How do you do? You're Frances Marion, aren't you?"

"Yes, I am. And you're—?"

"I'm Peg Entwistle. Oh, Miss Marion. I'm so honored to meet you. I have to ask. Doug, um, Mr. Fairbanks, thought you wouldn't mind. Would you write a screenplay for me like you did for Miss Pickford? You made her famous. I really need a job."

"It doesn't work that way, Miss Entwistle. You need to be under contract to a studio. And, please. I didn't make Miss Pickford famous, my dear. She did that for herself—with talent." She pulled away from this desperate, naive woman. How did she get invited to Pickfair, anyway? Not like the old days. Not by far.

A slight smile crept across her face as she turned away to see the four overstuffed chairs next to the glass doors where Harold Lloyd would perform card tricks for the guests before pulling out the Ouija board. Those were such good times. She gazed up at the massive portrait of Mary over the mantel that still dominated the room. It had been painted when she was at the peak of her fame. She was breathtaking.

She felt an arm on her shoulder and turned around.

"Hi ho, dear Frances. You look lovely tonight. How are you?"

"Hello, Douglas. I'm doing fine, thanks. And you?" She never really knew what to say to him. It was common knowledge that he was screwing every young thing on the lot. All those nights with Chaplin and the young girls. Mary knew about the others in Doug's life, but she didn't seem to care. It made Frances lose all respect for Doug, if she had any in the first place.

"Mary will be down in a few minutes. She's been getting ready for hours." His voice dropped into a hoarse whisper. "She's been drinking, you know."

Frances felt her spirits drain, but not surprised at his comment. Doug never approved of Mary's drinking, even in the old days. "The body is a temple," he would intone whenever anyone would listen. She thought about Bill back at the house and what he had said about the town drowning in booze. She hated it when he was right about anything.

"Oh. I didn't know."

"Yeah. Yeah," he repeated, absent-mindedly. "Sometimes I think these parties are just an excuse."

Frances was growing more uncomfortable with this conversation. His comments were cruel and quite inappropriate.

"I'm sorry," tumbled out of her mouth. She grabbed a drink off the silver tray proffered by an unsmiling, uniformed maid. At that point, she didn't care what it contained. This wasn't starting off well. She hoped this hadn't been a mistake. She moved to the bottom of the staircase and was tempted to sit down, lost in reverie, but didn't want to wrinkle the special electric blue gown she had selected for this night. Why had Mary invited her now, tonight, after all these years? Could it be that she was going to flash that coy little grin and tell her the marriage to Doug was over? Is this the night that she would invite her upstairs and…

An abrupt, raucous noise cut through the chatter. All eyes turned to the top of the stairs. The room fell silent. Frances looked up to see Mary, steadying herself against the dark wooden railing. With the floor-length puffy-sleeved yellow dress doused with beads and feathers, she looked as if she were headed to the junior prom – in 1910. But that wasn't the worst of it. Even from this distance Frances could tell those eyes that always caused such a flurry in her were blurry and a little sunken. The makeup was artfully applied as always but her face looked as if it had melted.

"You there!" Bracing herself against Mary's uncharacteristically strident call, Frances could sense the room around her battening down. "Frances! Is that you?"

Frances carefully modulated her tone in response, trying not to sound neither eager nor alarmed. "Hello, Mary. Yes, it's me."

"Frances?" She repeated, a little louder. There was a collective intake of air in the room. Frances was aware everyone was studying her, as if she might be held responsible for what was to come.

"Come on down, Sweetie." she said, smiling, encouraging her with a forced lightness. Frances could always buoy up Mary when she was feeling depressed or angry, almost as if she could reach inside her and toggle a switch. She started up the stairs to greet her, hope in her eyes.

"Noooo. You stay down there, right where you are." Mary gestured with her flapping left arm. What's going on? What's wrong? Where was her Mary?

"Frances!" she bleated again. "Why the hell did you write that script for Mary Miles Minter?"

No one moved.

It took her a second to understand what she was talking about. She tried to squelch her rising anxiety in a sea of reassuring appeasement. "Mary, dear. That was years ago."

"How could you write for that slut? And she killed Taylor!"

Frances knew Mary was referring to the still unsolved murder of director William Desmond Taylor. Minter had been one of the last to see him alive. Her career had fallen into the abyss from the scandal and the subsequent loose talk. Mary and Frances had gossiped about it at the time, but that story was passé and not meant to be polite dinner conversation. Why was she bringing this up now? And why was she so angry at her?

Frances' tone grew more pleading. She reached her hand upward in supplication. "Mary, please. Come down to dinner." She still hoped to salvage this spectacle somehow, even without the help from anyone in the hauntingly silent room. Frances was riveted on Mary up there on the staircase. She wanted so much to help but could not will herself to disobey.

The drama unfolded in slow motion as Mary unsteadily struggled to make her way down the lengthy marble staircase. Why didn't Doug go up there and help her? How she hated him at that moment.

Half-way down, Mary stopped. "Frances. Why did you do that to me? That Minter bitch was fucking my husband."

Frances' mind raced, trying to think of something to say, something to make this better, anything to make Mary love her again. Had Mary ever really loved Frances? In that instant, she knew she had to take a chance.

"Sweetie, please don't be angry with me. I would never do anything to hurt you. I love you. I always have." Astonished by what had just escaped from her lips, she hoped Mary would hear her, take her in, treasure her words like a sweet caress. She looked up at Mary, waiting for a response. Any response. When her words of vulnerability were met with thundering silence, she watched herself stepping back and shutting down, trying to protect herself by envisioning this as a two-shot in a film, where the famous writer is rebuffed by the fading movie star. In her wildest dreams, though, she would never have written this ending.

Her gaze sank from Mary's waxy face to the floor. Nothing could make this right or send her back to that splendid, simple time when she loved Mary unconditionally, wanted her in some forbidden, unspoken way. She felt lightheaded as she watched Mary return to an upstairs room. She was gone.

Breaking through the tableau of frozen guests, Frances turned and moved quickly toward the anteroom to find Morrison standing there without expression, holding her coat.

"I'm sorry, Miss Marion."

She reached for the coat from his outstretched hands and walked out the opened door where her car was waiting for her. The encounter had been like a choreographed dance, everyone familiar with its dramatic arc except the Academy Award winning writer who was left without words, the past muddled, her future uncertain.

Dinner with Daddy

She had forgotten how warm the rain can be in Los Angeles. Before she left her apartment on East 57th in Manhattan that afternoon, she had thrown on her ermine coat against the chill. The doorman had slipped on the ice as he reached to open the door of her town car. Now in L.A., the limo driver had his umbrella ready as she left the terminal and held it over her head.

"Welcome home, Mrs. Selznick."

"Thank you. This isn't home anymore." Since divorcing and moving to New York, her life had been on a strong footing for the first time. And it was her life, finally. No more controlling men who knew better than she did.

The driving rain obscured the sights out the streaked windows as they drove along Lincoln Boulevard. Irene was lost in her own thoughts. She couldn't remember the last time she was in the Bel Air house. She stopped thinking of it as home during her adolescence, after an occasional and furtive escape to see how other people lived. The Mayer estate had been more like a posh prison to her and her older sister, Edie, with whom she hadn't spoken in several years. "The Queen of Beverly Hills," Variety had called Edie – entertaining at her own vast Beverly Hills estate several nights a week and featured in the society pages of the *Los Angeles Times* nearly every Sunday. Irene had read about her father in *Variety*, of course. How his biggest stars were being released from their iron-clad contracts, how studio grosses were falling, how television was swallowing up the movie business. And Mother? Irene thought of her as the frozen, smiling palace guard, making sure everything was where it was supposed to be, keeping everything tamped down. Irene was hard-pressed to remember any opinions her mother expressed that were her own. There were the frequently recited "shoulds" about how to dress, how to speak, how to walk, and most important, the imperative to confide only in the family and no one else.

Irene didn't harbor ill will toward any of them. It was more detachment than resentment. She had walked away from all of them, even while she sensed the mountain of unfinished business. She had followed the rules, mostly, sampling real life when she could. But all that was ancient history. She was on a mission today. In spite of what was a shadow family now, she felt an unspecified obligation to them. Well, to her father, at least. She was bringing news. And she was late. That would be the first emotional obstacle to overcome.

As the limo turned east on Wilshire toward Bel Air, Irene reminded herself that it had been her father who invited her there for dinner that evening. As usual, her mother had called to deliver the message.

"Hello, darling. Daddy thought it would be wonderful if all of us had dinner together. Just like the old days. No husbands, no children. Just the four of us."

What an odd request, so startling she didn't think to ask the reason. She seldom heard from her father, in fact. They had met briefly after her play opened on Broadway, surprised that he had flown to New York to see her or maybe to take credit for it. Dinner at Luchow's was stilted, both of them involuntarily regressing to their familiar dinner table conversations – all about him and his business dealings. He hadn't said a word about the play. Nor had he called later after the announcement by the Critics Circle that the play she cast and produced had been nominated for Best Play of the Year. So why the command performance tonight? Is he dying? Selling the studio? Given the history, she chuckled, it must be about the studio somehow. It didn't matter. She had her own agenda. She had waited until the right time to deliver the news.

The limo maneuvered slowly up the driveway to the off-white mansion on St. Cloud, near the top of the mountain. She used to tell her one friend, "It was all the happiness money could buy."

"I'll take care of your luggage, Mrs. Selznick."

"Thank you." She didn't know this driver, but she had fond memories of the other help, the real people in her life growing up.

She walked to the front door and just for a second, hesitated. Should she knock? She had forgotten how forbidding and foreboding this place was. The neoclassical limestone exterior made it seem as if it belonged in another country, another century. She took a deep breath and opened the unlocked door to the imposing two-story entrance. No one was there but she could hear voices coming from the distant dining room. She forced a smile and walked toward the noise. All three of them were seated at the table among cocktails and hors d'oeuvres.

"Hi, everybody. Sorry to be late. The plane was delayed and the traffic on Wilshire was awful." She had learned early on to provide the excuses up front, forestalling the possibility of blame.

Edie, of course, was the first to pile on. "We've been waiting over an hour."

Mother recited her scripted lines, just like the old days. "It's all right, Darling. We're just glad you're here. Would you like a drink?"

"No, thanks, Mother. I had a nip in the limo."

She heard the familiar growl. "Hello, Irene. You're late. As usual." She reached over to hug her father. It was easy to maintain the distant A-frame connection since he hadn't risen from his chair. The tension was palpable before anyone said much at all, disconcerting since decades had passed since they all sat at this table. Like a bad movie, Irene mused, film noir. Certainly not an MGM production. They had to be bright and colorful with the inevitable happy ending.

Irene noticed that Edie had work done on her face since the last time they saw each other but that was logical, given how often she was in the public eye. She couldn't have her celebrity guests looking better than she did. Irene had to work to be cheerful with her sibling antagonist.

"And how's the celebrated Mrs. Goetz? No parties tonight?" Irene couldn't help the snark, a conditioned response. Edie merely smiled.

The server entered with the first course, a salad. Irene smiled when she saw him.

"Oh, Morton. I'm glad to see you. How are you? How're the kids?"

"Thank you for asking, Mrs. Selznick. They're all grown up. I'm a grandfather now."

"That's wonderful."

"I put a few extra croutons on your salad. Just as you like it."

"How lovely. You remembered. Thank you."

When Morton left, Margaret couldn't help herself.

"You shouldn't be so familiar with the help, Dear."

Then Edie echoed what sounded like a well-rehearsed line, spoken while bored. "They need to know their place."

Time stopped inside Irene's head. She could feel the oxygen thinning out and consciously struggled to deepen her breath intake. So this is how it's going to be.

"Oh, come on. We grew up with him. He's like family."

Edie quickly jumped in. "No, he's not."

Margaret leaned forward. "Isn't it nice that we're all together again? Just the four of us?"

This was the opening Irene had waited to hear.

"Yes. Why are we here, Daddy?"

L.B. barely looked at her, glancing up from the stack of papers to the left of his salad plate.

"I've missed you, Irene." He shoveled in another bite of salad, adding with a mouthful, "Oh, and you, too, Edie."

Same old Daddy. She knew she had been his favorite. Edie knew it, too, and it didn't sit well. Why did he stoke their sibling rivalry that way? These days, Irene assumed that her parents saw Edie often, since they all entertained the same A-list Hollywood personalities.

L.B. pushed the empty salad plate aside. "Remember when we'd go fishing off the Malibu pier? We'd spend the whole day together. Good times."

"I remember, Daddy. More like an hour. You were so busy."

"We'd talk and talk and talk. You were a good listener."

"Not much choice," Irene countered. "You never asked about me or my life."

He shrugged. "I didn't have to. I knew what you were doing. Where you were going. Who you were going with. I knew you wouldn't…"

"Yeah. I was just a kid, but I knew all the secrets behind the scenes. I loved that part. Whose little traffic accident was being finessed, whose wife was having an affair, who was gay…"

Margaret interjected. "You didn't tell Irene things like that, did you, Lou? She was way too young to hear that."

L.B. and Irene grinned at each other like co-conspirators. All that was a long time ago, she thought, and only a brief respite from the stifling and repressive conditions of her childhood. An oasis in the emotional desert.

"OK, Daddy. Aren't you going to tell us why we're here?"

The silence had lingered too long for comfort when Morton entered to clear the plates, returning a few minutes later with the entrée. For the first time since she arrived, she sat back in her chair and scanned the capacious dining room, larger than many people's homes. The table dwarfed the four of them, but the intent had always been clear: to keep everyone at a distance. The walls were covered with original paintings of the masters, the better to reflect the artificially cultivated values of the coarse patriarch, flamboyantly demonstrating his success. The room housed not one but two Rodins. Tonight, she realized for the first time it was like one of his movie sets. Everything was perfect. Except the casting.

Irene reconsidered how she would bring up her news. Should she wait until the end of the meal or defer until she heard her father's reason for the dinner? She didn't like to admit that there was still a part of her that felt like a child in his presence. He wasn't a large man, his face a stoic Rorschach, making him appear invincible and commanding, even in his own home. If his news was bad, she reasoned, she might not get her moment at all. Growing up in a show business family left her with an awareness of timing and staging.

Margaret smiled at her husband. "Look, Lou. Mildred prepared your favorite meal—beef stroganoff."

Irene knew her family was never short on irony. The daughters had been invited for some sort of mysterious special occasion, but the meal had been selected to please the boss. Why did she think it would be any different? There was something so predictable, familiar in its demeaning pathology. The sauce smelled good, though, the plate garnished just so.

L.B. suddenly pointed toward her. "You're staying here tonight."

Edie responded quickly. "Well, I'm not. I have a house to go to. And a husband."

Irene chose to ignore the slime on her divorced status. She had promised herself not to get distracted or get caught up in this again.

"No, not tonight, Daddy. I reserved a suite at the Beverly Wilshire. I have to get back to New York tomorrow." No reason to stay any longer than necessary. But now time was running out on this gathering and there had been no discussion of consequence. The air was getting heavier by the minute.

L.B. paused, gesturing with his fork in front of his face. "You know, you girls turned out pretty well. Edie, you're the best hostess in all of Beverly Hills. Like a movie star without having to work for it. Your house is like the goddamned White House. Everyone wants an invitation. And Irene. Well, you've surprised us all."

Uh oh. She opted for a decidedly lighter tack. "Because I divorced David?"

"No, no. Though I told you he was a no-good asshole. Never liked his father, either. Cheaters, liars, Pagans, Communists."

Cue the smoothing mother. "We don't need to go into all that, do we, Dear?"

Irene sat, waiting for the next line. She knew there was more. There was always more.

"Irene, you've become a successful producer. Who knew you had it in you?"

She was used to this backhanded praise. To dissect it would be too complicated and not the goal of the evening's mission.

"Thanks, Daddy."

Was this the opening she needed? She started to feel internal pressure, a sudden urge to bolt. Her heart increased its tempo and her mouth started to go dry.

She sucked in her stomach and began with simulated cheer. "I have an announcement."

Edie declared as if she knew what it was. "You're getting married again!"

"Absolutely not." She laughed, easing her own tension. "Better than that, I hope. And more permanent. I'm writing a book."

She looked at everyone's blank faces, one by one. Her mother predictably poured syrup over the portentous disclosure.

"That's nice, Dear. But I don't know how you find the time with everything else you're doing. You're so busy back there in New York."

Edie couldn't help herself. "What's it about?"

With his expected demeanor of certainty, her father signaled he knew by wagging his index finger.

"It's about me. Who better to write my biography than my own daughter? I could have the studio guys do it, but they'd get it all wrong."

Her breathing grew faster now. She felt frozen in the well-padded chair. When Morton came in to retrieve the plates, she careened between relief and impatience.

"For dessert, Mildred has prepared petit fours, Boston cream pie and chocolate cake. We also have vanilla ice cream, if anyone would like it."

Irene couldn't imagine eating any more. She had barely made it through the entrée, which wasn't all that good. Too heavy, like everything else tonight. She and her mother both declined. Edie asked for a piece of the cake. L.B., as usual, wanted it all.

"Just bring me a piece of everything. Ice cream on the side."

"Yes, sir."

As he left the room, Irene knew the spotlight was on her. Time for her close-up.

"Daddy, I'm sure your life would be a fascinating read, but I'm writing an autobiography."

Her mother smiled and nodded. "So it's about your father?"

Irene had learned to respond to her mother's limitations with patience. It was even more important tonight to keep it all as neutral as possible.

"No, Mother. Auto. As in self. It's about me."

Edie emitted an unguarded raucous guffaw. "Why would anyone want to read about you?"

Her father remained silent, studying the white tablecloth directly in front of him. It was perfect timing for Morton to deliver the desserts. If it had been a movie, she thought, there would be a loudly ticking grandfather clock.

L.B. dug into the Boston cream pie with alacrity. "Your years with Selznick could be a major motion picture – a horror movie. Great topic for a book. If it sells, the studio might buy it."

Irene felt some inner homunculus pushing her forward into the abyss.

"Well, the publisher wants stories from my life. My whole life." She tried out a chirpy laugh. "You know, people are fascinated by us. We're famous. At least, you are, Daddy. The editor wants to read stories from my childhood."

She wasn't prepared for the lingering silence. startled when Edie demanded.

"What did you write about me?"

Irene didn't want to be distracted by her sister just then. She had pulled the pin and waited for the full detonation.

Her mother fell back into her chair in a swoon, her words gushing forth in an accusatory way, but with her customary whine.

"Oh, Irene. How could you? Your father spent so much time and money managing what goes out of this house, haven't you, Lou? What will Louella and Hedda say?"

L.B. was still again, escalating the tension. It was uncharacteristic of him to edit himself or control his impulses. In a rapidly spewing internal dialogue, Irene worked to reassure herself that she doesn't live inside this family anymore. That she's nearly 40 years old, divorced with two children. That she's a successful Broadway producer. That she has friends, even a few doting men in her life. The deafening stillness was interrupted intermittently by the clanking of his fork against the plate as he devoured the pie.

Never one to absorb subtlety, Edie repeated herself, this time a little louder. "What did you say about me?"

Perhaps it would be enough to quell the unspecified threat, she thought. Maybe they'd settle for this. It was all about containment now.

"I wrote about how you teased me all the time about my stutter. I think you liked to see me cry."

As usual, Margaret stated the revisionist history. "Edie wouldn't do that, Irene. You two girls got along just fine."

Edie cocked her head to one side, like she did when she would tease Irene. "Rene, Rene, Rene, who s-s-s-s-stutters a-a-a-all the t-t-t-time."

Irene let her have that one. It only proved her point

"I also wrote about how you were the pretty one."

Margaret nodded. Edie was quick to agree. "Well, that part's true."

Now that she had delivered the news, Irene began to formulate her departure strategy. It hadn't been so bad, after all. She could feel her breathing returning almost to normal. And then he spoke.

"What else, Irene? About the family."

"Oh, I don't really want to…"

His tone grew more insistent, the one few safely ignored. "I want to know. What else?"

This was the moment she was dreading. She scanned her memory, trying to come up with something that would be prudent, long forgotten in the past, anything that wouldn't raise the temperature.

"Um. I wrote about how you wouldn't let me go to college."

She watched all three of them visibly relax. It had been just the proper disclosure, apparently. Oddly.

"I did you a favor. Girls don't need to go to college. You and Edie have done just fine without that bookish bullshit. Your mother taught you everything you needed to know."

"Thank you, Dear." Margaret seemed relieved.

Irene couldn't leave it alone. She wondered how long she could subdue the rising volcano. "But you wouldn't let me read books, either. I had to sneak off to the library after school."

Margaret in her reassuring tone added, "You're right, Dear. If I saw a book in your bedroom, I'd tell Mildred to throw it in the trash."

Irene wouldn't let her family know how appalling this had been to her, then and now. But she serendipitously had found the perfect example. Now if she could only find an exit line…

"What else?" the lion roared as he stuffed the remainder of the ice cream in his mouth.

She mentally reviewed some of the stories in the book, ones that could be considered neutral or even flattering. She knew about her mother secretly sending money each month to her father's older sisters when he wouldn't cough up a cent. That went on for years. He thought they were deadbeats, undeserving of their brother's largesse. Irene adored her aunts. No,

42

that probably wouldn't be a good choice. No reason to create dissent between her parents.

OK, she said to herself. She understood she was entering a minefield and would wonder later why she took such a chance. But there was one particular event she needed to discuss, a harbinger. She decided to lead into it slowly, shaping each word like a sculptor.

"You were strict with us in every conceivable way, Daddy, rules about everything – who we could talk to, what we should discuss, what we could wear. You wouldn't let us close our bedroom door even if we were alone. You didn't want us to be around boys or have friends outside the family."

She saw him nodding. "I was always thinking of you girls. You were my only concern. I treated you with no less care than I would my stable of shining stars."

Of course, she knew that wasn't true. It was seldom about their welfare. The only time he was home was for dinner. And then all he talked about was his day at the office. But that wasn't the topic here. Stay on track, she reminded herself.

"Remember the night you invited Charlie Chaplin over for dinner?" Irene pushed ahead, in spite of her better instincts. "I wanted very much to meet him. I loved his movies. I waited for that night all week. It's all I could think about. I wondered if I might talk to him about his work, but I knew I shouldn't. It would have made you angry."

Her mother smiled, reminiscing about what she thought had been a lovely evening at home. Margaret cooed. "Thelma called his cook to find out what he liked and made his favorite dinner. Veal scaloppini, as I recall it, with raw cauliflower and hollandaise. It was a perfect meal. Cocktails before. Didn't we have a string trio that night, Lou? After we dined, you took him into the den for cigars and brandy. It was a wonderful evening."

As usual, her father's impatience broke through, fracturing the warmth of her mother's words.

"Why would you write about that? It's shameful to use Chaplin's name to sell books, Irene."

In spite of the internal alarms, Irene continued. This might be her only chance, not only to clarify that evening but to warn her father of what was to come – in print.

"There was much more going on that night. First, Edie, you were all over him. You kept smiling at him, making goo-goo eyes, laughing too hard at all his jokes, sitting too close on the sofa. It was embarrassing."

Edie stiffened to defend herself. "I was being polite. A good hostess."

Again, Irene let this ridiculous assertion go. No point in getting distracted with family garbage. At least not this particular bundle.

"But the part that was confusing to me then, what you're all forgetting. He brought a guest with him that night."

Margaret bristled. Irene had sensed this might rile her, perhaps more than it would her father. "Oh, yes. That woman."

"Mother, it wasn't a woman. It was a girl. A teenager. She couldn't have been much older than we were."

Edie tried to get the focus off her attempted seduction of Chaplin.

"I remember now. She looked like she had troweled on her makeup. Drowned herself in cheap cologne. Clothes too tight. Whoa. How could I forget that?"

A funny little smile crept over her father's face. Irene had seen that expression before, as he sat behind his massive desk at the studio. He put on that smile when Garland walked in or when he looked at Lana Turner. His features softened.

44

"She was lovely."

When her mother spoke, it was so soft. It was almost a whisper. "They all were."

So many scenes flooded back in that moment, but Irene had to be selective. Say it and get out of there. "She was underage. After all your pontificating about right and wrong, lecturing us about proper conduct. It was confusing to me then. Not now, of course. I understand everything now."

L.B.'s voice suddenly grew louder. He banged his fist on the table. "I couldn't control who Chaplin brought into my home. He was a guest."

Seeing her father come undone in the austere dining room surprisingly emboldened her.

"Daddy, you controlled everything and everybody. This one seemed to slip through somehow. Why is that?"

She knew she was taking a risk, but it didn't matter anymore. Nobody confronted L.B., especially a woman. Especially his daughter.

"I wanted to sign Chaplin. His career had fallen into the toilet with the talkies. I could have had him for next to nothing. Why do I have to explain this to you? This is my family, not yours. Don't you ever forget that."

Of course, he had always made that clear. The family was merely the petals of a daisy with her father at the center. Her mother shifted uncomfortably in her chair. Her smile looked frozen in place as she spoke.

"Well, I didn't see anything. I thought we were just having a pleasant evening."

The family dynamics flashed through Irene's head like a movie trailer. Daddy was always right, no matter what. And Mother was half-blind to all of it. Irene didn't want to stop to comment, tempting as it was. There would be time in the book for that. She knew she had to finish this off.

"I didn't know what was happening that night, why I was so uncomfortable. I do now."

The silence was like white noise. Her words sliced right through it.

"Chaplin was screwing that poor girl. Or was about to."

Her father waved his hand in dismissal. "That's none of your business, Irene. Men will be men. You can't fight nature."

Irene understood, of course, these things happened in a business dominated by men where there seemed to be no ground rules. She didn't care about Chaplin's reputation for bedding young girls. She knew how the business of seduction worked. This was much closer to home. The non sequitur between that night and her father's sanctimoniousness was too dissonant to ignore.

Her eyes met his, black and cold. "Daddy, did you sign that girl to a contract?"

Once again, the scene was interrupted by Morton who entered with a whoosh. Margaret had likely pressed the bell summoning him from the kitchen like a 911 call.

"Would anyone like more dessert? Something else, perhaps?"

When no one responded, he backed out with the same velocity with which he entered. For an instant, Irene was glad the table was so large, keeping the family safely separated.

L.B. cleared his throat. Irene got a whiff of his aftershave, now wafting over the table.

"Irene. I won't discuss this with you. What goes on at the studio is not your business."

There had been many like that young girl, likely passed around. All part of being "studio property." But she knew her scene in tonight's family drama was almost over. It would be futile to continue and anything that followed would be awash with clichés. She rose to leave.

"Don't go." His forcefulness startled her. For a second, she hoped he wanted to discuss it, to finally break through the two-dimensionality of their relationship. He continued. "I have something to say to you. Both of you. Sit down."

Irene looked over at an alert and anxious Edie and noticed her mother staring into her own lap. She sat, thinking this to be perhaps her last act of obedience to her father.

"I called you both here because I want to say... Your mother and I are getting a divorce."

Irene's shock was mildly tempered by the awareness that she had been upstaged. "What? Mother?"

He cut her off. "It wasn't up to her."

Margaret spoke as if announcing the results of her bridge game. "It's true, Dear. It was your father's decision. It's been coming for a long time."

Irene assumed there was another woman or women. It had to be somebody special because her mother had endured his persistent infidelity over the years.

"Daddy, is there someone else?"

"Of course not. And it's none of your goddamn business."

Edie, roused from her stupor, swiveled her head back and forth between her parents. "I don't believe it. It can't be true. What will I do? What will people think? What will Bill think? What can I tell him?"

L.B.'s easily roused anger returned. "This is about the family, Edie. Not Bill. And not you. Jesus."

Irene watched Edie retreat, just as her mother had done all those years. Don't ask questions. And, above all, don't confront.

L.B. pulled his soiled napkin off his nap, threw it on the table and rose. "I'm going back to the studio for a while. I have a meeting with Dore Schary. Good night, girls. Good night, Margaret."

The three women sat stiffly in their chairs, their eyes following him out the door.

"I'm going home," Edie choked out. "I can't take this anymore."

When she was out of sight, Irene turned to her mother, a question in her eyes. Irene was suddenly feeling the weight of the evening, but she had to finish this conversation because these conditions would never be the same. Some invisible layer had been peeled away.

"I'm sorry, Mother. You did your best. I know that." Her mother merely nodded. "Aren't you angry at him?"

"Of course. A little. I knew about…his life outside the family. But I didn't know about her."

Irene longed to stop her mother's pain. "I've only put it together myself over the past few years. How you kept it all together, the family illusions, ignoring conflict. I always wondered why Daddy was the only one who was allowed to get mad."

Her mother nodded again. Irene had an idea. But maybe it was too soon. What the hell, she thought. She'd laid so much out there tonight already. She reached into her purse and pulled out a business card. She studied it for a few seconds and handed it to her mother.

"What's this?"

"This is my publisher's card. Just a thought. When you're ready, I'll bet you have a story to tell."

Margaret abruptly dropped the card on the table. "I could never do anything like that. It wouldn't be fair to your father."

Irene laughed. "Fair? You're concerned with fairness? Think about it while your lawyer is negotiating with his shark, while he's trying to screw you out of your life. You've never been on an equal footing. Can't you see that now?"

Irene got up, came around behind her and gave her mother a hug. "I have to leave in the morning, but I hope you'll come and visit me in New York any time you want. Good night."

She walked away from the dining room for what would be the last time. She turned around and saw her mother sitting at the massive table alone, staring at the card.

She did what she had come to do but she knew there would always be a need for further family excavation. There would be another chapter to write. No matter what, her father would land on his feet. Or someone else's. She was eager to return to New York where the weather was the only thing that chilled her.

Delayed Flight

I seldom travel alone these days. It's oddly quiet as I settle into my first-class window seat on the direct flight to LAX. No clever palaver from my understudy, no exchange of notes from my director, no script to memorize. Nice, really. To be honest with you, the isolation is anxiety producing, as if I only exist in the presence of others. Well, that's precisely what my last boyfriend said – that stupid casting director - and he wasn't around long enough to know anything about me. He was an egotistical jerk, anyway. He was wrong. So wrong.

New York is wonderfully distracting. There's always movement, noise, activity, challenge. It keeps my synapses firing without having to think very much. Since moving there twenty years ago from San Diego, my life has morphed into a world of the theater, what I always wanted. Talent has paid off. Definitely. And it will again, just you wait. That awful woman who stole the part from me will be revealed as untalented and they'll call me in to take over. She was shtupping the director. That's what my friend said. Well, yeah.

Jeez, they let anyone on the plane these days. Glad that woman with those two fussy kids isn't sitting anywhere near me. They're all germ factories. I wonder if I can take a nap. Uh oh. Here comes a doddering old lady. She's reaching over me to put her carry-on in the overhead. Should I help? Oh, good. The guy across the aisle is doing it. What's she going to do with the cane?

"Hello," she says, warmly, carefully lowering herself in the seat next to me. I nod. Oh, no. Hope it's not a talker. I don't want to be interviewed today. Since losing that Obie nomination to Agnes Purcell, I really haven't wanted to be around anyone. What were they thinking? It was clear my performance was better than anybody else's this season. Pure discrimination.

"Traveling alone?" Already she's invading my boundaries. Why does she care? Maybe she'll shut up once we take off.

"Yeah. You?" Gotta be polite. For now.

"Yes. I live in San Diego and my son is meeting me at the airport."

"Mmm."

Ah, San Diego. That brings back memories. Not good ones, either.

She looks to be about 75-80. Hard to tell. Those dowdy old-lady clothes make her look like she belongs in another century, that's for sure. Not much make-up, either. Why don't women realize just a little attention to themselves pays off? That face lift I had a few years ago was such a good decision. It took three cracks at it to get it right, but it finally made a difference. Even my mother had to take a second look to be sure it was me.

"Would either of you like champagne?"

I love traveling first class.

"Thanks. For sure." Always eager for that first glass.

To my surprise, the old lady takes one, too. Doesn't look like the type who'd drink anything but Martinelli's.

"Had a taste last week of Armand de Brignac Brut Gold. Ever try that?"

How would she know about one of the best bottles of the bubbly around? Don't they run around six thou?

"Uh, no. I prefer fine wines. Italian reds."

Wait. I should have said, "Yes" and it would have shut her up. Maybe if I just open my Kindle she'll take the hint.

"I'm Clara. Clara Shostic."

Oh, no. It can't be her. What do I say now? I know this woman. She doesn't recognize me, thank God. How long has it been? Twenty-five, thirty years? Oh, God. It's all coming back. She was the only drama teacher in that crappy little Podunk high school. What did she have against me, anyway? She put me in the chorus for "Pajama Game" when I should have been cast in the lead. What a bitch. I would have been so much better than that tramp, Shirley Kaufman.

I can remember the time she embarrassed me in front of everyone. I was in the middle of a scene for class and she threw an empty metal vase on the stage from the back of the room. She said she did it because she didn't think I was concentrating enough. I was so rattled that I couldn't finish the scene. It was awful. At least, I fought off the tears that wanted to come. I skipped my next class and hid out in the bathroom. Why would anyone do that to a kid? Vicious, that's what it was.

Then there was the time she told me…wait. What am I doing? I don't need to go down memory lane. Not again. I worked so hard to get rid of all of it. Of her.

"I'm Janice." She won't know my new name or my new face. God, I hope she leaves me alone. If I'd won that Obie, I'd want to talk to her, tell her what a success I am. How wrong she was about me. That would have been fun.

Ah, we're taking off. I'll just keep my eyes on the window, transfixed by the clouds. I guess I'm lucky to have been even considered for that Obie after the shitty experiences I had in high school. All her fault. I think some of the divorces were on her, too. She was the one who created my PTSD. Once I got from under all that, I was on my way. And here I am, almost on Broadway and in first class. Hmmm. What'll I have for lunch?

"Hello, ladies. Would you like the roast beef tostada or the chicken salad this afternoon? Oh. Excuse me, but you're Janice Sherman, aren't you? I saw your performance in 'Life Without' a few years ago in that little theater downtown. You were quite wonderful."

Shit. Outed by a stew.

"Thank you. You're very kind. I'll have the salad, please."

"I'm sorry about you and Mr. Sirokin. I thought you were so good together."

She could have just stopped with the praise. I don't want to be reminded about still another marriage going belly-up. It was dead after I met that sexy director, Peter, and we...

"I'll have the salad, too. A divorce? Are you an actress?"

Oh, jeez. Divorce equals actress, huh? Now what do I do? If we were near an exit door, I'd be tempted to push her out. She has no idea the damage she did. Some days I feel like I'm still picking up the pieces.

"Yeah, I am."

"I taught drama in high school for years. You look familiar to me."

Dear God. No. Does this window open?

Even as I peered into my Kindle I knew it was too late to save myself. But, hold it. Get a grip. You're grown up now. Not a kid. She doesn't have any power over you anymore. She can't insult you, make you feel like a nobody. You're not a nobody. You almost had an Obie nomination. The flight attendant recognized you. You've been on off-Broadway for a few years now. Well, off-off. You're on the way up, aren't you? You met Angela Lansbury. You've...

"I had a student years ago who looked a little like you. It couldn't have been you, though. Shelley was mousy and you're very glamorous."

Mousy? Mousy? Did she say mousy? Who was mousy? I might have been a little shy but never, ever mousy. What an awful person. Is there any way I can stop this? I had wanted to avoid an interview, but this feels more like an interrogation. Everything but the rubber hose.

"Funny thing about Shelley, though." She was looking at me more carefully now, turning sideways in her seat to get a better view. "She had genuine talent. That's hard to find in high school drama."

What? Now she tells me. I'll bet she knows. Dammit. She knows. What's happening here? I feel caught, like I'm still in the 11ᵗʰ grade and got found out while smoking in the girls' bathroom. I'm going to keep up the façade. Hold on. You can do this. Did she say I…uh…Shelley had talent?

"She did?"

"Yes, she did. I think she wanted me, needed me, to tell her how good she was, and I decided that wasn't the best thing to do for…for her."

Here comes the rationalization for being such a destructive bitch.

"People like that with lots of talent, you know, can get too comfortable. They're young and they get dependent on others instead of relying on their own…well, on themselves."

How can I find out more without getting in too deep here? Why the hell do I want to know more? Wish the restroom was empty.

I can't help myself.

"What do you mean, dependent on others?"

"She had to find out for herself how good she was. Now, looking back, I was probably too critical of her in class."

Aha! She admits it. Well, that's something.

"Too critical?" I try not to smile or look smug.

"Yes. But she had to learn how to be her own critic, not be so vulnerable to others' opinions. I wonder if she ever learned how to do that."

I don't want to look at her. The flight attendant saves me.

"Here you go, ladies. Two salads. Would you like a glass of wine with that?"

Almost as one, we chime, "Yes, please." It's the first time I don't feel a sense of high-altitude rage at the teacher I thought had been way too eager to plow me under.

As we work on our food, I want to hear more. Sort of. Until now, I hadn't realized how much this – she – had bothered me, affected me all these years. I decide to take a chance.

"What would you say to…Shelley… if you were to run into her today?" I can't believe I'm asking that. Careful here.

"You know," she says, buttering the other half of the tiny roll, "Teachers are a lot like parents. We want the best for our kids, but we make mistakes, too." She was looking right at me now. I think she's apologizing.

"I understand."

I can feel something inside give way. Like loosening a belt. The defensive wall I had put up years ago? I still feel so protective of that frightened teenage girl who wanted so much, too much maybe.

I'm continuing to rewind that old movie in my head. The pimply-faced, overweight kid who wanted to be on the stage, the kid nobody liked. The kid who wanted the acceptance she never got at home but never fit in. The kid who felt rejected by this teacher. She was right. She did make a mistake with me, but she was also right about it making me stronger. Did I imagine it, or did I feel my face lose its tension? I need to think about this.

I pick up my Kindle and sense I'm on a different kind of trip, like finding the solution to a long unsolved puzzle I didn't know was there. She's right, though. I still care way too much about what people think. Especially men. Dammit. I'll call my therapist when I get home.

The Last Fan

She used to be Joan Davis. Now she was just another 53-year-old has-been living behind tall, well-manicured hedges on Tamarisk Road in the Palm Springs area known as the Movie Colony.

Nobody knew who she was anymore, surprising since she had been in the public eye since hitting it big in vaudeville as a young girl, even playing the Palace more than once. Later, there were dozens of movies during the 1930s and 1940s. So what if they were on the second half of the bill? Over 30 million people listened to her on the radio every week. Her NBC television show was good enough to last three seasons, though she existed in the shadow of the higher-rated Lucille Ball, whom she deeply resented. There was even an Emmy nomination. But none of it mattered now. She could walk into the Milton F. Kreis drug store on Palm Canyon and nobody even looked her way. Now she was by herself, except for her maid, Lorena, still with her after all these years. The only one who stayed.

Sometimes she felt comforted by the framed playbills, the movie one-sheets and the dozen or so 11x14 glossies that were neatly lined up on her hall wall. On her bad days, she could always find a reason to retrieve something from the back bedroom down that hall of triumph, just to reassure herself who she once was. She was no longer fond of looking at herself in the mirror, but those airbrushed photos made her look almost beautiful.

These days, she spent more of her time on the welcoming, forgiving couch, staring at a droning television set. What was the matter with people? It's all just shit now. So much had happened since her series was cancelled six years ago in 1955. TV was funny then. She was funny then.

"Miss Davis? Would you like something to drink?" Lorena knew the answer but kept up the pretense that it was still a choice.

"Yeah, thanks." She was studying the man on the little screen. "Lorena, do you watch Jack Benny? It's OK. You can tell me."

She paused just a second before she answered, checking her boss' face before setting the drink on the table. "Oh, sometimes, Miss Davis. He makes me laugh. And I love Rochester."

"He's good. Knows his pacing. Went to school in vaudeville like I did. Jack was always wonderful to me. I wonder why he doesn't have me on his show."

"I don't know, Miss Davis."

Of course, Lorena knew. She overheard the desperate phone calls, the pleas to producers. She had overheard her boss asking that nice Mr. Cantor to help her get back on TV. Not many people wanted to work with her anymore. She was temperamental and demanding, they said. Others weren't as kind.

"I'm going to call Eddie."

"I'll be in the kitchen if you need me."

She straightened her dressing gown, lifted the receiver off the black phone and dialed the number by heart. She and her Eddie went back at least twenty years. Maybe even longer than that. Two tough vaudevillians from the schools of hard knocks and coarse living. They spoke each other's language, though he was 15 years older. She had never worn heels around him so she wouldn't tower over his diminutive stature.

Whenever she heard his high tenor voice, a smile crept over her. "Hi, Lover. Can you come over?" There was a pause on the other end.

"Ida's here this weekend. Can't, Joanie. I'll give you a call early next week. Yes?"

He was always so solicitous. She understood he had to keep up the façade of the marriage. He couldn't very well abandon Ida now, after making Ida and their five daughters a standing joke for years in his act. Joan endured the frustration if only because he found her gawky frame sexy and her rubber-bodied antics endearing. She didn't regret a minute of being with him. He made her feel loved. Life would be so much nicer if Ida would find her own lover or just drop dead.

"Don't worry. I'll be fine." She didn't want him to feel guilty. "Call me when you can."

Carefully, slowly, she replaced the receiver in the cradle. Speaking to Eddie always unleashed a tide of wonderful memories. She remembered working with him on those routines in that movie, "Show Business." She had wanted to be good for him because his money was in the picture. Singing and dancing with him were the best times she could imagine. At least, she had the movie one-sheet framed on the living room wall to remind her how good she was. She looked at it all the time.

"Lorena. Another, please."

"Coming, Miss Davis." Joan had lost count, but Lorena kept tabs. Joan didn't understand why she did that and it annoyed her sometimes. Maybe it was just habit. There had been falls, after all, nothing serious. Following a particularly heavy night of drinking after watching Ed Sullivan, she had almost set the couch on fire when she fell asleep with her cigarette burning. Still, if Lorena paid attention to the vodka supply by keeping track, that was just fine. It was an essential part of her job. Joan was enraged when she didn't get her glass full when she wanted it.

"I'm going to leave in a while. Is that all right?" Joan wished Lorena could live in so she wouldn't leave her alone at night. But it was just a two-bedroom house and Joan needed the other bedroom for her daughter or her mother when they came for their infrequent visits. Half of the spare room was filled with her performance wardrobe from the old days, anyway, the dresses and costumes locked away in dusty plastic designer bags. All ready for her comeback.

"Sure. Don't forget to lock the door."

Joan watched her leave, then made her way to the kitchen where she poured herself just one more before settling back down on the couch. It didn't matter what was on. It was all shit. Even "My Little Margie" was better than "Car 54, Where Are You?" Wonder whatever happened to Gale Storm, anyway. She was convinced Gale's show was only popular because it had followed "I Married Joan."

Peering through the back windows in the dark, she couldn't see the pool she knew was there, surrounded by grass kept green and trim by the weekly gardeners. It was important to have good help. She liked living here. If only...

In some ways, the house itself was an apt reflection of her dismantled state. She had started with antiques but in the middle of last year, she took a liking to the mid-century look becoming so popular in Palm Springs. Nothing matched but everything had been expensive. She liked being rich. She fell into a hypnogogic sleep, revisiting the hard times working in those seedy theaters, waiting her turn to go on for the sixth time that day. She hated it when there was an animal act just before her. Without much effort, she could bring back the pungent smells of flop sweat and greasepaint. Even now, she doused herself each morning with My Sin to help blot out her olfactory memories. She had remembered getting up to go to bed but hadn't noticed the time. It didn't matter. Not much did.

She was awakened by the sound of the doorbell and her two French poodles barking their strident soprano arias. The second more insistent wave of ringing told her Lorena hadn't come into work yet. She found her dressing gown and stumbled to the door.

"Eddie! You're here." She stepped forward as he extended his arms. They were just about the same size. How convenient. She always noticed how handsome he was - when he wasn't mugging for laughs. She didn't care that he wasn't wearing his hair piece, either. Or that he was there so early.

"I came as soon as I could. Ida went back to Beverly Hills this morning." He led her into the living room where they sat on the couch. "What's wrong, Sweetie?"

Though she trusted Eddie more than anyone else in her world, she never felt safe telling anyone what she was feeling. People hurt you. They take advantage. She hadn't been successful by relying on others. Her show was in the top 10 because she took control. She'd done it all herself, like it or not. Nobody gave her credit, either.

She looked directly into his intense brown eyes. "I need to find something. That pilot I shot a while back about me being an astronaut never got off the ground." They both laughed at her accidental humor. It was serendipitous when that happened as neither was as funny as the personalities they presented on the screen. Comedy was serious business, seldom infusing their personal lives. "My production company has folded. Nobody wants the 'I Married Joan' films. When syndication ends, so do I."

"They will, Sweetie. I gave you some ideas before. Have you talked to anyone at Revue or General Studios?"

"My agent is supposed to make those calls, but I think he's down for the count. I don't make him any money these days." She gestured toward the kitchen. "Would you like a drink?"

He shook his head. "It's a little early, isn't it, Joanie? Come on." The phone ringing made both of them jump.

Lorena would be late, she said, hoped it wouldn't be an inconvenience. Something about a problem at home. She got off the phone and smiled at Eddie. "We all have problems at home, don't we?"

She knew Eddie didn't like to talk about his domestic situation. He was here now and that was enough. No questions. No complications. Nobody noticed when they purchased their respective homes in Palm Springs within months of each other, and a few minutes apart by car. Not those bitchy gossip mongers, Hedda and Louella, certainly, and more importantly, not Ida.

"Why don't you do a book? Mine has sold pretty well. The ghost was careful about leaving out the drecky times and people. Nothing about our personal relationship."

She grinned. "You don't think it was between the lines? Or sheets?" She loved throwing innuendo at him. "So why don't you? You'd have the control you want."

"I don't know that I want to go back there. Lot of bad times, ya know? And I sure couldn't do it myself."

"You won't have to. Let me give you Jane Ardmore's number. She's a little stuffy but that's not a bad quality in a writer."

She shook her head. "Well, I don't…"

He smiled and leaned toward her, taking her hand. "I remember the first time I saw you." Joan knew what was coming. He always brought up this story when he was trying to sway her. She loved hearing it and inhaled a nose full of his English Leather. "You were third on the bill. Not bad. I was next to closing. You wound yourself up and skidded all the way across that stage on the heel of one shoe. How the hell did you do that? As many times as I watched you, I could never figure it out."

She smiled, loved the memory of that act in particular. "It always stopped the show, didn't it? Took me months to learn how to do that without busting my ass." They shared another laugh.

After Eddie left, Joan stood in the shower, flooded with memories. The bad relationships, the abusive marriage, the endless hours of hard work, the loneliness, the resentment she felt from the men on the TV show, its cancellation after only three years. It was hard to hold it back. But, she reassured herself, she had a closet full of furs, a new car, this lovely home in the Movie Colony. Even her daughter seemed happier now. Maybe Eddie was right about the book. It would help her focus on the good times.

She zipped up her slacks, pulled on a loose top and combed her hair away from her face. She hoped Lorena had left out some bread so she could at least make toast. Even though she wasn't doing those outlandish and dangerous physical stunts any longer, she managed to keep her weight down without dieting. A liquid dinner had its advantages.

It was 10:30 already. Where was Lorena? The doorbell rang simultaneously with the toaster's ding. The yapping poodles ran to the door. Damn it. It's probably just another fan. Oh, wait. She knew that wasn't true. There weren't any of those now. She still didn't understand what happened. How did it all disappear so fast?

She moved the dogs away from the door and took a step outside into the portico and closed the door lightly behind her. Standing a few feet away was a mailman, actually a young woman in a crisp post office uniform. Even with the desert heat, she looked well-pressed.

"Yes?" Joan wasn't sure quite how to handle this kind of thing. Lorena always answered the door, took care of the service people.

"Oh. I'm sorry to disturb you, Miss Davis. I have a package for you. It wouldn't fit in the box."

"Fine. Thank you, dear." She took it and started to step back inside.

"I hope I didn't disturb you. I didn't expect to see you."

"I live here."

She stammered a bit, studying her feet. "Yes, I know. I've been on this route for almost a year, um, hoping to meet you."

She looked at this woman, a girl, really, for the first time. No beauty, that's for sure. She was short, had what looked to be leftover acne scars and clearly enjoyed her desserts. She seemed almost vulnerable standing there on the porch.

"Well. That's very nice."

"I loved 'I Married Joan' and I was so sad when it went off the air. You were...sensational and hilarious."

Joan wasn't used to this. Even when she was on the network every Wednesday night, she seldom gave interviews and didn't go out in public much. And now after all these years, she had to remember how to bring back that phony magnanimous celebrity demeanor that had once come so naturally. She was out of practice.

"Thank you. And what's your name, Dear?"

"I'm Donna. I know that's your real name, too. Madonna, like the saint. I'm Catholic, too."

Joan had to laugh. She hadn't thought about that name in a long time. And it had been even longer since she had felt like a Catholic.

"You're absolutely right."

"And I know you were born in St. Paul, that you had a popular radio show on CBS, that it was sponsored by Lever Brothers, that you were in lots of movies with Eddie Cantor and Abbott and Costello and Milton Berle and Alice Faye and…"

"You're quite a scholar, aren't you?" The vaguely acerbic tone couldn't cover the fact she was touched by this woman's words and breathlessness. "But you're far too young to remember all that."

"I read all the fan magazines. You can probably tell. Oh, I'm going on too long. I'm sorry. I do need to get back to my route. And I know you must be very busy." She started to back away from the threshold then turned to look at her once more. "This has meant a lot to me. You know, I see lots of famous people on my route, but you…." The final word seemed etched in the air. Joan's eyes moistened over, in spite of herself.

"It's been nice talking with you, too, Donna. Thanks for the package."

She closed the door behind her and felt an unfamiliar wash of adrenalin. She was at her best in front of a large audience; these one-on-ones were inevitably uncomfortable. Still, Donna was so fresh, unguarded, genuine. What a great way to start the day. She finished her toast and poured a shot of wake-up juice, tossing it back in a single gulp. If only that kid had been a part of the Nielsen family, she thought, I'd still be on the air. She turned when she heard the front door open.

"I'm sorry, Miss Davis. I'm so late."

"What happened?"

"It's the husband. He's sick again. I don't know what I'm gonna do with ole Leroy."

"Well, you better figure it out. I need you here."

"I know, I know. I'm sorry." She put her things in the closet. "What can I get for you?"

Even her maid was about to abandon her, after all this time. Damned husbands. They always screw things up.

"Just a short one. Good enough for now."

She sat for a minute, took a sip of her breakfast, then went to the phone book. She found the number for Bullock's and dialed.

"Hello. This is Joan Davis. Joan Davis. D-A-V-I-S. I have an account with you. For a long time. I would like to re-order the yellow silk lingerie set you sent me a few months ago, but in blue. I also need a set of linen sheets for a double bed, in white, please. Yes, same address. How soon can you deliver it?"

A few mornings later, she got up with the sun streaming through her windows, performed her familiar daily rituals, and idly wondered what time the mail would arrive. She went to her usual spot on the couch in the living room after turning on the TV to watch the morning soaps. It was embarrassing how engrossing those could be. She wouldn't be caught dead on one of those, though, no matter how much she missed working. None of them was funny, ever. Not an ounce of humor anywhere. And terrible acting.

At the commercial break, she gravitated to the front windows, the ones facing the street and the mailbox. Lorena was sweeping the back porch and hosing off the outdoor furniture. Standing at the window, she could hear Lorena chatting with the pool guy. There was a sharp yell and a loud splash, then another. She hurried to the back yard in time to see both Lorena and the pool guy standing in the pool, each holding a small white dog.

"Those goldarned dogs got into the pool again, Miss Davis. Are you sure they can't swim?"

Her fear was nearly mitigated by the funny scene before her. Both adults waded to the edge of the pool and carefully placed the wet dogs on the deck. Joan stood at the edge of the pool and tried not to laugh. It reminded her of her debut in that Mack Sennett comedy back in 1935. Mack kept reshooting her scenes in the water. She had been terrified but there was no union to protect actors back then.

"I wouldn't want to take the chance. Thanks, you guys." She turned to the rescued piles of wet fur. "Bad babies. Bad! You need to stay out of the water. It's not good for you. And you know Mama can't swim." She loved those little dogs more than anyone. Well, except for Eddie.

Emerging from the water, Lorena grabbed towels from the cabinet near the back of the pool.

"Come here, you little rascals. I'll dry them off, Miss Davis. I turned my back for a short minute."

Joan returned to her vigil by the front window. There she was at the curb by the mailbox. Joan walked outside, pretending to look for something in the driveway. And, actually, the box from Bullock's was right there on the doorstep. What luck! Donna saw her, gave her a big smile and walked over to hand her the mail.

"Hi, Miss Davis."

"Donna. How are you doing today?"

"Oh, I'm fine. Wow, here you are again. Hey, I was thinking. Remember that episode where you have to tutor the football kicker from your high school alma mater? You were trying so hard to be nice to him and gave him all those pastries. He got so fat the coach ordered him to lose weight. And you helped. You were so funny, wrestling with all that gym equipment., falling off the bars. Didn't you ever hurt yourself on the show?"

"Lots of times. Tons of broken bones but please don't tell anyone. I had to make it look easy. We had a nurse on the set all the time and she was busy, let me tell ya."

Lorena passed by them on her way to the store. "Be back soon."

Donna noticed the box on the doorstep. "How about I help you carry this big box into the house?"

"You don't have to do that. It isn't really mail, ya know."

"I know. Happy to help."

"Right over there is fine. Would you like something to drink?"

"I'd sure love a Coke. It's hot today."

Just as she retrieved a Coke from the fridge, she heard a splash.

"Uh oh." She ran outside to see both dogs in the pool. Where was Lorena? Donna followed her outside.

"Can't they swim? I thought all dogs could swim."

"No, they can't. And neither can I. My babies. Oh, oh, oh, my God."

Joan looked around for something like an inner tube, a pole, anything. Then Donna bounded feet-first into the pool, hurrying over to one dog and shepherding her to the side. Joan watched as her other precious baby appeared to struggle to stay above water while Donna jumped to the other side to get her. Joan could hardly breathe.

"Here they are!" She came up to the edge of the deck, smiling broadly.

"You got them. You bad dogs. I have to sit down. This is too much. Twice in one day. That damned Lorena left the back door open again." She pointed to the towels by the edge of the pool.

Donna laughed. "Well, I said it was a hot day, didn't I?"

"Thank God you were here."

"See? They don't seem to care, do they? Guess they wanted to cool off, too. I'm glad I could help. Listen, I have to go home and change before I can finish my route."

"How can I thank you? I'm so grateful. Please take the Coke with you. It's the least I can do."

Donna negotiated her way to the door, hopping over the stark white carpeting in the living room. She turned and reached to shake Joan's hand, but Joan drew her close, giving her a warm hug. Joan surprised herself at the atypical gesture.

"Thank you, Donna. Thank you. Thank you." Joan pulled away quickly, always embarrassed by any show of affection unless it was with Eddie. And even then.

How ironic that this woman, a mailman of all people, would be here just now, at the perfect time, and that she would be such a big fan, too. She asked nothing in return, either. Joan realized she could have offered her an autographed photo, but she was too overcome by the close call to think about such niceties. She maneuvered toward the vodka, hoping to calm herself down. As time passed, she felt more angry than scared. She couldn't very well fire Lorena, but it just goes to show that you can't really trust anyone these days to do their job.

She settled herself on the couch and dialed Eddie's number.

"I've had such a morning. You wouldn't believe this." She unraveled the whole saga for him - the meeting the other day with Donna, her sweet worship of Joan and the incredible luck that she was in the house when the dogs nearly drowned.

"That's quite a tale. Lucky, indeed. Listen, Joanie, Ida's coming back this afternoon, so we can't get together for a couple days."

"I understand. Sure wish she'd get tired and divorce you. You know what I mean." She missed him so much when he wasn't there. He had become a part of her life and wellbeing, more so over the years.

"That won't happen, Joanie. You know that. There too much at stake for both of us in this marriage. We fight but she has no grounds. A divorce would be brutal. She could ruin me. Us."

"I know. So much for 'Ida, sweet as apple cider.'" That had been a running joke between them for years. Eddie's theme song had long been a hollow tribute to his mythical wedded bliss.

She and Ida seldom met and that was for the best. Now that there were no more films, there were no excuses to get together. Joan and Eddie had to be more careful. They hadn't been seen in public together in years. Eddie came over only when Ida was out of town and would leave before Lorena arrived for work. She was sure Lorena knew what was going on but, at least on this subject, Joan trusted her discretion. Eddie was all she had, really. And maybe Donna. Maybe.

Joan couldn't envision a real friendship with Donna, whatever that meant. She was at least three decades older than Donna. All they really had in common was that they were members of the Joan Davis Fan Club. But that was just fine with both of them, it would seem. Joan found herself waiting for the mail delivery each day so she could invite Donna in for just a minute, just long enough to stoke the embers of her ego.

On Lorena's morning off, Eddie often spent the night but would be gone by mail delivery time. When the doorbell rang one particular morning, Joan and Eddie were having breakfast, Eddie in his boxers and a tee shirt, Joan in her robe. Joan rushed to answer the door to find Donna there, grinning like a schoolgirl.

"I have a package for you, Miss Davis."

She was surprised to see her, two hours earlier than expected.

"You're early today, Dear."

"I know, Miss Davis. Hope it's OK. Lots of extra packages to deliver today."

"Sure. Don't you think it's time for you to call me Joan? Thanks. I'd invite you in, but I have a guest."

"I can see." She peered around Joan to see a man sitting at the kitchen table. "Isn't that Mr. Cantor?"

"Yes, he just stopped by for a few minutes to discuss a new film script. Would you like to come in and say 'hello?'"

"That would be exciting, but I can't. I'm covering an extra route today. I'd sure love to see you both working together again. Maybe another movie? See you tomorrow, I hope."

As soon as she left, Eddie smiled at Joan. "I'm clearly not as popular with her as you are. Guess I don't rate. It would be swell if that were true, wouldn't it? That we could work together again?"

"I'd love it. Maybe a tour to promote our books. I did call Ardmore to talk about it and we're meeting next week. What a great excuse to be together. After all, we're big in each other's books. Professionally. Co-stars to the end!" she waved dramatically.

"I'm pleased you're going to do it, Joanie. Let me know if I can help. I need to get a shower and get out of here. As always, thanks." They hugged each other tentatively. As close as they had been, Joan was still uneasy with physical contact. Still, she wished they could return to the bedroom if only to keep him there longer.

Joan looked at her watch and saw it was a few minutes past the time for her favorite soap, "Search for Tomorrow." She poured herself a drink and sat down in front of the TV. Before long, Lorena would be there. She had leaned on her heavily about the dogs getting out, and she had promised to be more careful. Somehow Joan knew she would be. For the first time in a long time, Joan felt at peace, more settled. The autobiography would return her to the public eye. It would give her lots of plausible time with Eddie and now, after all this time, she had an honest-to-goodness fan. Donna's daily visits gave her something to look forward to, like a vitamin infusion, bolstering her in so many ways.

There were still those long nights, though, when she lounged alone on the couch, half-heartedly watching crap on TV while finishing off a bottle. Will they ever get tired of showing those stale Westerns? Their flimsy plots made it hard to turn off her mental rehash - all the inequities, the slights, the disappointments, the rejections. She had been so good, better than Lucy, better than any of the men at physical comedy. Only Chaplin came close. She knew she had never been a beauty; she had to be funny. It came naturally to her from the very start. Now, nothing was easy. But it was getting better, wasn't it?

The days melted together through the unseasonably warm spring. The weather was perfect, but Joan found it hard to get off the couch. Eddie came over when he could. With his support, she had set up a schedule to meet with the ghost writer. The highlight of the day, though, was always the arrival of the mail. Joan ordered things she knew would require a door delivery from Donna, giving them a chance to talk for a few minutes. Now and again, Donna would come in for a Coke. Those were good days for Joan. If only Donna were a writer, she could help her write her book, the perfect combination of knowledge and adulation. But she knew Donna wasn't all that educated and that she was barely able to make ends meet, even with her post office job. She had refused any financial help from Joan, which had surprised her. She'd only taken an autographed photo and those Cokes.

It was after 11 on a Saturday night when the doorbell rang insistently. Ding, ding, ding, ding, ding. She had been dozing on the couch, lulled by vodka and the boredom of "Gunsmoke."

As soon as she opened the door, Eddie rushed in, his trademark banjo eyes popping like he was under attack.

"She knows. Ida knows everything."

"What? How? Sit, sit. Take it easy." Joan was still trying to rouse herself from her deep sleep.

He looked as if he might explode so she perched on the other end of the couch, providing a cushion of safety for both of them. Eddie took a minute and sucked in a few hyperventilated breaths. Joan watched him carefully, wondering how he felt about this development and how it might impact their lives together.

"First, Joan, Sweetie, pour yourself a drink. You're gonna need it."

Joan obediently went to the kitchen and poured each of them a tumbler of booze.

"What do you mean?"

"She kicked me out. She's called her lawyer."

"Jeez." She felt an excited jolt at the back of her neck. She thought this could be good news in time.

"This is the real crapper. You know how she found out?"

Now Joan was leaning on every word, thinking that that this might mean Eddie would finally be hers. She could move all the furs into storage, making room for....

"It was your sweet little mailman."

Joan couldn't quite take this in.

"Who?"

"That fawning little fan you keep talking about. It gets better."

She couldn't find words, much less formulate a coherent question.

"Ida has been paying her. Her lawyer thought it up. I don't know all the details. It doesn't matter. But Ida was screaming at me that it had cost her a lot to get the goods on me. I guess your 'fan' needed the money. Or something."

Joan put down her glass. "I don't believe it." How could she have been so wrong? It didn't make sense. The bottom fell out of her stomach. "She knew all about my career. She loved the show. She remembered the plots."

"My guess is that asshole lawyer gave her all the ammunition. I'm sure she doesn't give a shit about anything but the money she made ratting on me. On us."

She thought of all the good talks they had, the look of awe in Donna's eyes when Joan talked about working with her co-stars and with Eddie. Oh. She was trolling for information, even then. But she had jumped in the pool to save the dogs. She saved the dogs! All part of the set-up? A lucky coincidence?

"I feel like such a dope."

"Don't. She was a good actress. She played you like she had done this before."

"I don't even want to think about that. I don't know what to do. What do we do, Eddie? Tell me. How can we make this work for us?"

"I need to deal with Ida. I can't let her divorce me. This can't happen. It would be the end of my career. And I don't want my girls to find out, either."

"What about me? Isn't this a chance for us to…?

"Joanie, you know I love you." He moved closer to her, but she pulled away.

She persisted. "You can stay here. Don't go to a hotel."

"No, no, You know I can't. We have to stay away from each other for a while until I can get her back on track. It's happened before so I have an idea about what I have to do."

"What? What's happened before?"

"It's not important, Sweetie. I need to call my attorney, figure out how to make this go away, how to keep her quiet."

There was a palpable silence in the room.

Joan felt as if all the bones in her body had turned to liquid. She couldn't think. She couldn't feel. This isn't real. What just happened here?

"You go to bed, Joanie. I'll get back in touch when things calm down. And good luck with your lying mail bitch."

She didn't look up to see Eddie leave. There was a loud noise in her head. How alone she felt at that moment. She swore to herself that she would never answer the door again, resolved to never trust Eddie in the same way. Things had morphed into completely unfamiliar territory. She had to think, to plan. She flashed back to the interview she gave when the network had announce that "I Married Joan" had been canceled. She told the young writer not to worry about her, that she would get along just fine, as she always had—on a mixture of "gall, guts and gumption." She always loved her clever phrasing. She'd need all of it now.

She stiffly lifted herself off the couch and shuffled over to the kitchen cupboard. She hoped Lorena had remembered to reorder her regular weekly case.

Deconstructing Doris

She was feeding the dogs in the cook's kitchen when she heard the distinctive roar of his Porsche breaching the silence as it pulled up in the circular driveway in front of the contemporary house on Crescent Drive in Beverly Hills. She hurried to the front door, opened it and walked to the car to see Terry's grim face.

"Mom, he did it. You're dead broke." He shifted his feet and frowned. "And you owe the IRS. He took it all."

Doris Day never expected to hear those words, not in her worst dreams, and certainly not from her son. She stared into his eyes for a minute, hoping for a disclaimer, a joking response, anything to mitigate the shock.

"But how…"

"I don't know. But it looks like they've been screwing you over for a long time."

"They? Jerry and Marty?" She had barely spoken Marty's name since his death the year before. She had often thought back to when they had met almost 20 years earlier. She had signed a contract with Warner Bros. but when she met agent Marty Melcher at a party at Johnny Mercer's house, he convinced her they weren't paying her what she was worth. Within weeks, they were in bed together, personally and professionally.

Over the years, he had guided her career, her life, really. He was the caring Svengali she always wanted, someone who loved and protected her from the show business sharks. It didn't bother her that he jumped aboard as an Executive Producer on her films when he didn't do a thing but collect his check. She trusted his opinion about what she should record, though he lacked any musical training. Her precedent-shattering triumph as a top ten box office star for ten consecutive years told her he had done a wonderful job. She knew people didn't like him, considering him a bossy moocher, a guy who needed to order people around. When she heard a director on one of her films call him Farty Belcher she laughed in spite of herself. She didn't care so long as the money and movie parts kept rolling in and she could record at Columbia, her favorite place to be. At least he didn't beat her like Terry's father did. And he obviously wasn't gay like her second husband. Why couldn't she get this right? God knows, she had enough practice.

All those years on the road with the band on the bus, men grabbing her, teasing her, trying to get her into bed. Sure, she enjoyed some of it, but it cost her along the way. When Marty came along, he was strong and sure and exactly what she needed. She was relieved and grateful. To succeed in the business, she had left the distraction of raising of her only son to her mother. Having Marty come into her life as a co-parent gave her a feeling of family she hadn't often experienced. She didn't have much of a childhood herself. Her mother saw to that, putting her in shows at an age when little girls were playing hopscotch. When Marty came long, it seemed a sure thing that Terry would have it better than she did. They would all be all one family now.

She trusted him. Loved him, at least early on. He and Terry didn't get along, she knew that. But he had adopted Terry at a propitious time when the kid was young, an angry and rebellious adolescent. Looking back on it now, she could see that it gave her new husband more leverage over her. For Doris, it solved the unspecified ache. There were times when the guilt about leaving Terry behind with her mother was almost unbearable. Marty was a solution to an empty heart in several ways.

"You were right about him, Terry. I didn't believe you."

"He hit me, yeah, but it's nothing compared to what he did to you. I want to kill him."

"Yeah." She was still trying to put this together. Terry could be wrong. She knew he was back into drugs again, hanging with dopers. She worried about the influence from his new stringy-haired girlfriend, too.

"It'll take a while to figure out how much is involved." Terry's jaw crackled with tension. "Could be as much as twenty-thirty million. Maybe more."

The money is gone? How could they have afforded this house, then? The beach house? She had never wanted for anything. Marty made sure of that.

"Wait a minute. He hit you?"

"Yeah. Lots of times."

Her mouth fell open. She reached for his arm. "Why didn't you tell me?"

"You were never there when it happened. You were working. It wasn't your fault." She looked for a shadow of resentment in his broad, open face so much like hers, and saw none.

"Oh, God, I'm so sorry, Honey." She reached out and hugged him, but the emotions could no longer be contained.

Doris ran into the house and threw herself into the soft confines of the down comforter on the king-sized bed and started to weep. Without thinking, she drew closer to the four King Charles spaniels nearly buried there. Thank God for them, she thought. She didn't want to think about Terry being abused but, if she were honest with herself, she never wanted to hear anything negative about anything. She didn't like feeling bad. She was busy working—at being a perfect performer, a perfect person. Everybody thought she was. Sometimes, even she believed it. In spite of Marty's bellicose ways, she knew she was loved by the people she worked with, by those who worked for her, and even more by her fans. She was a nice person. How could this happen?

Reaching for the Kleenex, she smelled the sweetness of the gardenias floating in the bowl next to the bed. Dear Barry had sent the flowers just the day before. Barry was a sweet man, not at all like the others. When she'd finished dining at the restaurant where he worked as a maître 'd, he would bag up leftover bones for her dogs and they'd chat about his dog. The ambrosial aroma of the gardenias offered a faint and fleeting whiff of hope.

She couldn't get the glowering image of her dead husband out of her head. "I won't let him get to me again," she said aloud, surprised at the stridence of her own voice. She was stunned at how real Marty's presence was in her life even now and how he could still devastate her. She looked up as her housekeeper walked into the room. "It's OK, Sarah."

"Are you all right, Mrs. Melcher?"

Doris recoiled at hearing the once-beloved name but nodded. She didn't want to upset anyone.

"I can bring you a glass of…something, if you'd like."

"I'm fine. Thanks." She watched Sarah silently back out of the room.

Doris was almost 50 now, the years wearing well on her. She had people come to the house every morning to do her hair and makeup, and to help keep her slim body in shape.

The helpers had become trustworthy friends, people she could count on. They were good company. Looking in the mirror was sometimes difficult but that wasn't new. There were always those damned freckles which seemed to spread like grains of sand on a windblown beach as she got older.

She looked out the window toward the manicured back yard and stared at the crystal-clear water where the pool man was energetically vacuuming the bottom of the pool, creating waves that splashed over the sides.

The memories kept coming. She felt stupid and somehow responsible for what had happened to her, struggling to make sense of it.

When Terry stuck his head in the door, she continued the conversation as if there had been no pause.

"But why Jerry? He and his wife spent all those weekends with us at the Malibu house." There was a plaintive edge to her voice. "He even got along with Marty. He was my lawyer, too, for God's sake. He handled that last divorce. He was a pit bull. Marty trusted him, too."

"I know, Mom. I know. Maybe too well. But he was the big financial guru, remember. He was the one with all the advice about investments. He had to know. Maybe he set it all up."

The mood momentarily brightened. "You think it might not have been Marty's fault?"

"I know you want to believe that, but he was involved. Jerry never made a financial move without Marty's OK. Dammit, they were in this together. You have to accept that."

She knew she had to stop romanticizing him as the sculptor who molded her career, the good guy, the one who made the best decisions. Up to now, she could separate out the husband from the agent and manager. Her perceptions of her life with him, however, were transforming right before her eyes.

Her mind was racing, a collection of flashbacks and scenes. That conversation with Judy Garland during a serendipitous meeting on the train to New York ten years ago or so. Funny how that comes roaring back now. Judy had loudly complained about her husband, whom she felt was using her. Doris had defended Marty. He would never take advantage, at least not that way, and wondered why Judy had laughed. She had enjoyed the talk, though, glad that Marty and Sid had gone to the club car hours ago for drinks. Neither man was what you'd call handsome. Both were dark and stocky, with coarse features. And both had been their third husbands, men who fancied themselves professional kingmakers.

It wasn't often she had the chance to get together this way with someone she admired in spite of the much-publicized problems. Doris didn't do drugs, not much alcohol anymore and didn't understand Judy's addictions. She liked her and that's what counted. Judy made her laugh. And she knew how it was to work for a tyrannical studio boss, the relentless and dehumanizing pressures. With Judy, it had been Louis B. Mayer; Doris' nemesis was Jack Warner. They laughed as they shared horror stories.

"He would actually get on his hands and knees on the plush carpeting in that garish white office and tell me he was begging me…as a father," Judy chortled. "The poor old guy could get it from anyone on the lot. It was pathetic. I tried so hard not to laugh. Fathers don't try to shtup their daughters." They both doubled over with laughter, gasping for air.

Doris had stories, too. "Jack was a total jerk, always, always hitting on me. Those beady little eyes. Marty started coming to the office with me. Gave me protection. We both learned how to play the game. And it wasn't so bad, was it? We got what we wanted, didn't we?"

Judy became more somber and looked away. "Sure." Doris wondered what she was thinking as she turned to study the speeding landscape. Doris could see Judy's face darken in the reflection of the train's window. What was Judy not telling her? Had she missed a warning?

To be fair, she had known Marty was a cheater and a liar when she married him. He had been married to one of the Andrews sisters when they met. She remembered one frightening evening when they were in bed. There was an insistent pounding on the door of her apartment. A woman was yelling outside. Doris was terrified.

"Shhhh," he whispered, quietly reaching for her hand.

"Let me in, you bastard. I know you're in there with that slut. Come out here and face me, you asshole."

Neither of them moved. How did she know where Doris lived? Were they followed? In time, the screaming stopped, and they heard the footsteps slowly fade.

Then there was the recording career. Marty had his fingers in everything she did. Some said he deliberately commissioned only second tier songwriters to write her songs, saving money. For the good of the family, she thought. She never complained because she loved the music and the musicians, but now she understood the money went somewhere else. And those last movies weren't the best, either. He had convinced her to leave the safety of Warners and selected the rest of her films himself. How could she have let that pass? Her career mattered to her, a lot. She comforted herself by thinking of the warm relationships with her wonderful costars. The often-inspired pairings kept her spirits high and her career on track, in spite of the lousy dialogue and contrived plots, especially toward the end.

Her stomach clenched as she realized it was all her own damned fault. She had lived her life on automatic pilot, delegating it all, riding on her innate talent. Whatever was going on with Marty was in the background. There were more pressing issues almost all the time.

There had been her mothers' long decline into Alzheimer's, which took its toll on everyone. Then there was Terry's increasing drug use and his skanky friends. And the Humane Society that kept coming around unexpectedly to count the number of animals she had. That made her angry. It was easy to lose track, she'd claim. She was doing a good deed, after all, taking care of all her homeless four-leggers. She had been sick, too, really ill for a long time until she talked Marty into letting her see a doctor. The hysterectomy, done in secret, away from prying public eyes, waylaid her for months. All that was nothing compared to the pressure of maintaining her wholesome and cheerful image, her stardom and the health of her glorious voice.

Whenever she got anxious about money, Marty reassured her. "Everything's going well, Doris. Jerry and I have this under control. Relax. We know what we're doing. These investments will pay off big and very soon."

Yeah, she had been used, but she had to give herself some credit. She pushed for a separation a year or so before he died. There had been a long overdue confrontation, but it wasn't about money.

"I know you're seeing someone. Who is it?"

"Doris, it's nobody you know."

"It's never nobody. I don't even know what that means."

"It didn't mean anything."

"It never does, to you." She held in most of her anger. "We're done. I'm sorry but I can't do this anymore." She glared at him. "You have to leave."

Within a month or maybe two, she had started to see other men. Her friends told her not to rush into anything, that she needed to figure out who she was as a single person. And while she felt free, she was also afraid - of making her own decisions, of another mistake, of managing her own life. She had never been alone, that is, without a man. Now she could spend time with friends and not have to check in constantly. She rode her bike all over Beverly Hills, resting only briefly in the local park where she almost always ran into smiling fans. It made her day.

It didn't bother her too much that Terry had moved out of the house a few years back, eager not only to start his own life but to get away from Marty. He was living with his girlfriend on Cielo Drive in Bel Air and life was good for him. Terry told her he wanted to be a record producer, so she got him a job at Columbia Records. She was glad for his success, but she missed him. They still talked on the phone almost daily, exchanging gossip and sharing the absurdity of life, more like friends than mother and son.

She remembered finishing a guffaw-filled lunch with a friend, an old Warners colleague - or "inmate" as they joked - at her favorite deli just a mile from her house. It had been several years since they'd seen each other, but when they sat down their affectionate bond was immediately rekindled. They left with a promise to get together again soon.

Wheeling her bike into the slow traffic on Beverly Drive, she heard her name.

"Doris. Hey."

There was Jerry Rosenthal, their attorney, waving at her from across the street.

Jerry parked quickly and leaped out of his car. He looked agitated.

"Marty's been taken to the hospital. In an ambulance."

It had to be serious for that to happen. Marty had more than adopted her Christian Science beliefs. He had co-opted them, refusing medical treatment for anything, even with the acute pains he was having. She had no idea.

She stopped everything after his hospital discharge, even taking him back to the house on Crescent Drive where they had once lived together. She thought she was through with him, but there was still unfinished business. The cancer had spread and there was little time left. She hoped they could talk about, well, everything, but he was too weak and not at all interested in resolution. She persuaded him to hire a nurse and tried to convince him to eat. He got thinner, complained constantly and she watched him die. She had felt guilty only briefly, regretful of all she had not done for him, could not do. But now, in the light of this new shocking news, she was glad he suffered, glad he was dead. Even the good memories were gone.

Her reverie was interrupted by the phone, unaware that two hours had elapsed since Terry came home with the news. Terry entered the room and picked up the receiver.

"It's Jerry."

She felt a whooshing inside her head.

She turned to Terry, who was still holding the phone close to his chest. "What should I do?"

It was so hard to break that habit, that reliance on the men in her life. This was not the time for reformation. She needed time to think.

"You don't have to talk to him. I'll take care of it."

She sat back down on the bed and reached for her golden retriever, tenderly scratching him behind the ear. "I don't know what to do. I don't understand any of this."

Terry nodded to his mother and spoke into the receiver. "Jerry, don't ever call here again. Our attorney will be in touch."

Attorney? Of course. That would be the solution. At least, one of them. She would sue Jerry for whatever he stole. Could she report him to the police? Could he go to jail? How will she live now? Where's the money? How could this happen? Marty?

So many questions, but she knew two things. First, she would sue the shit out of Jerry Rosenthal. And second, she was convinced that the only man she would ever trust again would be her son. Well, maybe Barry. Such a kind man.

The Curtain Never Falls

Each night, she waited to hear the door open, the narrow beam of light moving towards her as she lay in bed. Most nights, she didn't mind. Other nights, she resented the intrusion into her deep reverie.

She saw the silhouette of the care worker.

"Miss Bose," she whispered, with a soft Cuban accent. "Oh, did I wake you? So sorry. Is everything all right?"

"Yeah, Carmela. I'm fine. Good night."

"You just call if you need anything."

She heard the door close then turned on her right side, toward the darkened parking lot outside her two-bedroom apartment. There was just enough illumination to remind her of the ghost light, that eerie dimness on stage after the audience has gone home. She loved performing. It seemed to quell the neediness for an hour or two, rendering her fully alive. In that quiet time when it was over, the afterglow was unforgettable. She often stood on the deserted stage as the electricians above her rechecked the lighting and the stage manager retied the riggings on the scrim. Then, as now, the melancholy would dissolve into memories of a life lived in front of strangers.

What's the cliche? "Hold them in the palm of your hand?" That's what she did. Her broad, buck-toothed smile, her arms outstretched to embrace the entire audience - her world, really. She kept time by twisting her zaftig body from side to side. She possessed them, hypnotized them with her talent and her asides that sounded unscripted, in that rough-and-ready, raspy voice. Critics said she was a dynamo, "Exuding enough energy to light up New York City," they said. It wasn't that long ago, was it?

The final appearance had been at the auction of her household goods in West Los Angeles on a rainy Friday morning. In truth, it had been over well before then. As the years piled on, she grew more fragile, couldn't muster the catalytic energy which had been the hallmark of her act. Then one night at the late show at the Holiday Inn in Paducah, she had fallen down the stairs. And after another fall a few years later, at 91, the bones stubbornly refused to heal. She resisted using the wheelchair as long as she could, but she knew she had to accept it.

She didn't like to think about the career slowing, because that's all it was. A time out. The audience never forgets a star no matter how many years go by. One of her finest performances was at that very auction when she didn't shed a single tear over her prized possessions going for pennies on the dollar to her fans and to memorabilia collectors. There were those little ceramic figurines of comedy and tragedy she kept on the kitchen shelf next to the stove, the salt and pepper shakers of Amos and Andy, the Christmas serving plates she had collected for decades. The older she got, the more sentimental she became about these little touchstones, trinkets that reminded her of her past glories. They were reassurances she was a beloved person, someone with a welcoming house full of tchotchkes. The men - and the husbands - came and went, but the house belonged to her alone.

It's gone now, providing enough money to stay in this upscale assisted living facility until she's ready to go back on the road.

Encinitas Gardens is a newish building, two stories of contemporary architecture, a *porte cocheré* framing the modest front entrance. She was mostly confined to her wheelchair when her daughter brought her there for a reluctant look. The facility was spacious, bright and clean and the people seemed nice. One even remembered who she was.

"Oh, Miss Bose. My mother brought me to one of your shows at the Grand in Dubuque when I was eight years old. We sat in the third row. I can picture it as if it was yesterday. I felt as if you were singing just to me."

"Well, I was, Dear. What's your name again?"

"Melody Springer. Let me show you around. There are several two-bedroom units available. I'm sure you'll find something you'll fall in love with."

Maggie Bose turned to her daughter standing behind her and shrugged. She hadn't wanted to do this. She thought she had earned the right to die in her own house, the one she and her first husband bought right after the war. It wasn't a mansion; just a modest three-bedroom, tract house in the San Fernando Valley. But she had to refinance it so many times that the meager residuals couldn't cover the mortgage any longer. Or much else. After repeated falls, she couldn't manage herself, either. She would never ask her daughter for that kind of help. Never. She had raised her to be an independent woman, just like her mother. But things change. They always do.

When they entered one of the apartments that overlooked the parking lot, her daughter, Adelaide, spoke up.

"Mother, you'd love this. It's very bright, isn't it? Lots of light."

"Yeah."

"And you could watch the cars come and go."

"Yeah."

"And look. You can put your piano in this other bedroom."

"Yeah, I could." The sullen silence was palpable.

Adelaide turned to Melody and smiled.

"We need to think about this, I guess. Thank you for…"

A seasoned performer, Maggie knew when it was time to get off the stage, when the act was over.

"No, no. It's OK. I'll take it. It'll be fine."

The coming weeks and months felt like a prison sentence. Oh, the other residents were friendly and the staff helpful. If she wanted food, she had to maneuver her wheelchair down the hall to the dining room three times a day. The food wasn't bad, but the setting was disquieting. A melancholy twinge inevitably overcame her as she waited for her order. The indiscriminate low hum reminded her of the impatient sounds an audience makes while waiting for the curtain to rise. One day at lunch, a woman about her age tottered up and studied her face.

"Didn't you used to be Maggie Bose? I remember going to see you in vaudeville when I was a child."

"Yes, I am. You have to remember, I was just a child, myself."

"Oh, sure. I remember. You had such a powerful voice. Especially for someone so young. Do you still perform? I mean, when you're not here."

Her face assumed its public smile, though she dreaded any questions about her show biz days. It was like an electric current shooting through her. It had happened often enough now that she had a well-rehearsed answer.

"I don't work much these days. My fans are still out there, though, so it's possible you'll see me on the stage again very soon."

Her inquisitor smiled and nodded and returned to her four-top across the dining room.

Maggie's practiced demeanor faded along with her appetite. Without waiting for dessert, she wheeled herself down the hall and back to her apartment. The first thing she spotted was always that baby grand piano. It hadn't been used since her arrival six months before, but she still hoped to locate a local musician who would accompany her, to prepare for her next gig.

Her only child, Adelaide, had come to visit the day before, bringing her fan mail. Some of her old television appearances were still being rerun late at night. Those who watched associated her with their own good times, long gone, when life was simpler and easier to manage. She still got a couple of fan letters each month, sometimes from people in other countries. She was sure her fans would come to see her again, once she regained her strength.

Her daughter had only stayed for a few minutes, which had become her custom. Her presence always elated Maggie, especially when she'd bring along the letters.

"You know, I lie in bed at night going over my act. Just to keep it fresh, you know?"

"But Mother, you don't really expect to work again, do you?"

"Oh, sure. I'm thinking about a way I can work from the wheelchair. Honey, I know I'm good."

"You were. You really were. No doubt about that. The best in the business."

"I figured I'd take a pay cut just to be able to work. Brad might not be happy with me about that. He was always sure to get that 10%. I think it's important to keep up the chops."

"You know, things have changed in the theater. Vaudeville's been dead a long time, you know."

"I know that. I didn't leave the stage. The stage left me. There are lots of clubs out there that would love to have me as their headliner. I can still fill a room."

"Yeah, Mother. Yeah. Well, I need to go."

"Thanks for the mail. And thanks for coming. Love you."

"Me, too."

She sometimes wondered why the facility hadn't asked her to perform for the other residents. They always brought in outside talent. She decided it was because they couldn't afford her fees. Still, it might be fun some time. Nobody does a good act anymore, certainly none of the amateurs they bring in here. Most of them were amateurs, lacking in polish or presence. She wouldn't have to do the whole act; just a couple of songs she knew would bring down the house.

Even after six months there, she had difficulty making friends. Throughout her life, her pals had been other performers or those who worked for her. Almost everyone she liked had died. She didn't know many civilians, didn't know how to talk to them. Sometimes, during the increasingly frequent hospitalizations, she was uncomfortable kibitzing with the nurses and aides. What do people talk about, anyway? At Encinitas Gardens she would take her meals with other people, most of whom talked at her, expressing little interest in who she was or who she had been. It made her feel hollow and abandoned.

In fairness, she knew there was an edge to her personality, a wariness that came from years of being disappointed, screwed over and victimized, but it never got in the way of her giving her usual upbeat performance. When she was out there, it was balls to the wall, all the way. She needed her audience in ways she could not describe and her connection with them was electric. Why didn't it translate to this place? Why didn't they want her?

She spent most of her days in front of the television set, watching old movies or reruns of shows that weren't very good the first time. Her once Technicolor world had suddenly flipped to black and white. It's not fair when the mind is still sharp, she thought. It's the body that won't work. She knew she would find a way, convinced an eager audience would welcome her back.

A year went by without much change. The 911 meat wagon was a regular caller at Encinitas Gardens, often many times a day. Residents came and went, frequently disappearing due to death. A staff person came in every week to clean, and to wipe away the dust from the top of the unused piano that continued to serve as a daily reminder of her loss. The ennui was numbing. She started to lose track of the days and even the time. Someone whose name she could never remember came in the morning to deliver her meds and that same person knocked on her door to remind her when it was time for dinner. Hallmarks of an empty life.

A few months back, she heard a comedienne had moved in, just down the hall. She had been on a popular TV show for several years, so everyone knew who she was. Maggie had met her once or twice in passing, so one morning after breakfast, she went to her apartment and knocked. A woman with bright orange hair answered the door.

"Maggie, is that you?" Florence leaned over her the wheelchair and gave her a big hug.

"Hi, Florence. I heard you were here."

"Yeah. Not for long, I hope."

Maggie laughed. "That's what I thought, too."

"But the wheelchair…"

"Oh. Broke a bone but I'll be back on stage soon. I'm sure of that. What about you?"

"That's right. You were a stage performer, weren't you? A club act. Not in TV or movies."

"No, no. I did a lot of TV. Don't you remember, 'Millie's Family'? I had a recurring role as the next-door neighbor."

"Oh, yes. Now I remember. It's too bad that show only lasted one season. I thought it was pretty good."

"But why are you here?"

"You know, I'm almost embarrassed to tell you. My house in Bel Air is being renovated. My business manager wanted to put me up at a hotel, of course, but I thought I'd take this opportunity just to get everything checked out. You know, us old broads aren't as healthy as we used to be."

Maggie stiffened at the denigrating term.

"How long will you be here, then?"

"Not more than two-three months, I would guess. It would be fun to get together and share some old times, wouldn't it?"

Maggie had never cottoned to Florence, thought she was full of herself. And, to be honest, she didn't have a lot of talent, either. She couldn't sing or dance. She just recited lines on a TV program. Anyone can do that. She was funny because of the writers, not because of any inherent sense of humor.

Maggie forced a smile. "Sure. That'd be fine. I'm pretty busy working on my new act right now but I'm sure we can find time. Maybe at a meal."

"Yes. I think the food is pretty good here."

True to her prediction, Florence wasn't there long, and Maggie was relieved when she left. She had learned to time her meals so that Florence was sure to have left the dining room. She didn't want to see those old people flocking around her, asking her silly questions about that dumb TV show. They were just making fools of themselves, sycophants, not real fans. Probably demented, too. There were lots of those here.

One afternoon, she decided it was time to put in a call to her agent.

"Hi, Brad. It's Maggie."

"Maggie."

"Maggie Bose."

"Oh, sure. Hi. Maggie! Nice to hear your voice. Haven't heard from you in a long time. How are you?"

"Well, I've been busy. Actually, I'm staying in a care facility for a while. Temporarily. I was wondering if you could find some kinescopes of my TV appearances. I know it's hard to believe but these people don't…well, I guess they didn't watch much TV back then. I was thinking it might be fun for them to see one of their own on the screen."

There was an awkward silence.

"Maggie, that was a long time ago."

"I know, but there must be…"

"You can't even find kinescopes these days, Honey. But some were probably transferred to videotape or were digitalized. Once in a while, you can still find one or two on late-night TV."

"Could you check for me, please? I think it would be a kick to see myself again. I mean, for my friends here to see me in action. You know."

"Sure. I'll look into it. Oops. My other phone is ringing. Nice to hear from you, Maggie. Take care."

It must have been around two in the morning. She had finally drifted off to sleep with the "Mannix" rerun droning in the background. The loud ringing startled her awake, like a fire alarm. Isn't it a little late for a drill? There was heavy pounding on the door.

She recognized the voice of the night aide.

"Everybody out. Fire! Fire! Stay calm."

She slipped on her robe, lowered herself into the wheel-chair and navigated toward the door. The smoke was beginning to fill the hall, causing her to cough. She knew she had to get out quickly. She could feel a sharp pain in the leg that resisted rapid motion. That smell immediately reminded her of the fire at the Alcorn in Buffalo. That old vaudeville house was a firetrap and one night, right after she finished her act, she heard someone yell, "Fire!" She found herself surprisingly calm in disasters. She knew what to do.

"Help me, please! Help! Help!"

That sounded like Gladys, her fragile next-door neighbor, whom she knew was unable to function without help from the staff. Where were they? Was she still stuck in her bed? Wasn't anybody going to help get her out?

The cries grew louder and more desperate. She figured the thickening smoke had likely filtered into Gladys' apartment, too. Maggie called out for staff, but no one responded. Dammit. This place is always understaffed. She wheeled herself over to the phone and called 911.

"There's a woman trapped in her room, 478, I think. It's a fire. Someone help her." She was so frazzled that she forgot to give her name, the name of the center, or the address.

The cries were intense, frantic. "Please, please. Help!"

Maggie threw a towel over her mouth and headed down the smoky hall to her neighbor's apartment. The door was un-locked, a fortuitous oversight by a careless staff member.

"Maggie! Help me! Please! I gotta get out of here!" Glady was crying, which only escalated the coughing.

"Hey. It's OK. Can you sit up?"

"I'll try."

"Boy, you're just a bag of bones. If you can, lean yourself over my chair and…"

"Wait. Oof. I'll inch towards you."

"Better hurry, Sweetheart. We don't have all day."

With every bit of strength both of them could marshal, Gladys laid herself across Maggie's lap. They say in a crisis, adrenaline kicks in. Maggie wheeled the two of them out-side via a side door, both sputtering from smoke inhalation. Once they reached safety, they grew quiet, breathing heavily in the far reaches of the parking lot for what seemed to be a long time.

"Gladys, you're going to have to find a way to get off me. It's safe now." The pain she could ignore during the rescue was unremitting.

Gladys looked at her. "Weren't you scared? You seem so composed."

"Listen, Honey, I've followed bratty kids and trained seals on the bill. After that, most anything is a walk in the park. We got out OK, didn't we? Nothing to worry about."

The sound of sirens and diesel engine trucks filled the air. Two firemen rushed over to them.

"Are you ladies OK? Do you need an EMT?"

Maggie looked over at Gladys now lying on the grass.

"I think we're both OK. You might want to check her out, just to be on the safe side."

Gladys pointed to her new friend.

"She saved my life. I would be dead if it weren't for her."

The firemen gently guided the two of them to a remote spot in a grassy area away from the buildings, one carrying Gladys in his arms.

"Please stay here where you'll be safe. This will take a while. Looks like the whole wing is going up. We'll knock it down. Don't worry about it."

Maggie thought about her piano, her arrangements in the file cabinet, the two fan letters she hadn't yet answered. More losses. And another place to live. She didn't like change of any kind.

Hours passed, the women sitting mostly in silence in folding chairs on the grass. They could see the fire and smoke dying down, but the acrid stench would take longer to dissipate.

Maggie had nearly fallen asleep in her chair when she opened her eyes to see a TV reporter coming toward her followed by a cameraman. She wished she had a mirror and had taken the time to dress and comb her hair.

"I'm told you brought this woman out on your wheelchair. Is that right?"

Gladys answered quickly.

"Oh, she did. She did. She's a hero. She saved my life. She's wonderful. I'm going to tell everyone. She was like a superhero in a Hollywood movie."

Maggie smiled slightly, her eyes following the camera lens tilting toward her good side. She still knew how to pull focus. Some things never fade away. The reporter took a longer look.

"Aren't you...didn't you used to be...that singer? Um. Maggie Bose! Right? My grandmother was a big fan."

She looked down with faux modesty. "Yes, I am. Still am. Not was."

Gladys couldn't resist a comment. "And she was very good, too. Think of the courage it took for her to do what she did for me."

The two women retold the events of the rescue several times for the other reporters who had gathered around them - the fear both of them felt, the relief at inhaling the clear air in the parking lot, the sadness that their apartments were likely gone, the bond that had been created between them out of this disaster.

The local newsman was reassuring. "The rest of the complex looks like it was untouched. I'm sure they'll find you another place pretty quick. No one wants you to experience any further inconvenience. Especially you, Miss Bose. You really are a hero."

Gladys again, spewing the words out with gratitude. "I'm sure all of you will want to interview her, won't you? And your colleagues, too"

"Yes, indeed. My cameraman will get your names and… well, we already know yours, Miss Bose."

When the interviews had concluded, an Encinitas Gardens employee moved both of them into the safety of the larger building. Wheeled past the burned-out ruins, Maggie could see that this would make a wonderful Movie of the Week. They could easily find someone to play Gladys. And, of course, she would play herself. She would call her agent in the morning.

Madelyn, Mostly

The trouble started on stage, as might be expected. Being good mattered more than anything to her. For a while, she tried to figure out what was wrong, how she got off track this way. Now it had gone on too long.

Madelyn loved singing those sentimental old songs, the ones that had words that meant something. Not the rhythmic crap you hear today. As a performer, she was best known for those melancholy ballads that would tear your heart out. Even as a kid, she could weave her warm personality around those lyrics and grab an audience. And sometimes, she would use her musical language to relate to others, especially men. Words, after all, could be tools of seduction. But in recent years they had become something more - neurological inroads, ways to relate to herself and not always in a good way.

My schemes are just like all my dreams,

Ending in the sky

The intrusion of random song lyrics had never been troublesome before but now they had become like refractive lasers into her subconscious mind, information she wasn't always open to receiving. There was no warning, either, causing disruptions in her concentration and well-being.

She had never been this nervous before any performance, at least not since she was 12. But this was something else. Riding in the car with Helen, her personal assistant, Madelyn hoped it wasn't anything serious. After all, she wasn't crazy.

All your fears are foolish fancies, maybe

"What's the address again, Mad?"

Madelyn reached down to smooth her skirt as the car pulled up to the traffic light. It would have been better had there been more flexibility to get to the appointment, but it takes time to get ready for any appearance.

"It's on little Santa Monica, just past Beverly Glen, I think, 10935. Wish we were going out to lunch or something. Or, even better, a rehearsal."

Madelyn reached for the mirror in her purse and checked her face again. She never left the house unless everything was perfect and, indeed, it was this day. The wig had just been freshly coiffed, the double set of eyelashes firmly affixed, the blue eye shadow just so. It took longer these days to create Madelyn Mercer, carefully filling in the cracks and crevices of a long and sometimes dark life. You never knew who you might run into, maybe even paparazzi or some eager fans. The oversized sunglasses on her face would protect her identity for now. There was too much else to think about.

She heard Helen's voice, "You sure you want to go through with this?" Helen had worked for her a long time and didn't like her to see her like this, anxious and unsure of herself. She had grown attached to this selfless woman who seldom complained, even after those occasional outbursts of temper. It was easy to take her for granted. Twenty years younger and dowdy in demeanor, she was the perfect assistant.

"I don't think there's much choice. At the Bowl last week, I forgot the lyrics in the middle of three different songs, even

"Cabaret." And there were those flashbacks again. Why is this happening now, Helen? Jesus, you'd think at my age I'd be done with all that. I don't do drugs or drink that much. It was my husbands who were the drunks."

Madelyn looked out the windshield to see the freeway jammed ahead and was glad Helen was driving, as she always did these days. Maybe it was her encroaching age, but Madelyn had no patience for much of anything now, least of all, any performance problems.

"Being a legend is hard work," Helen teased. Madelyn knew her easy tease was a time-honored way to get her to relax. She appreciated Helen's attempts. Today, however, the comment was lost in the noise of the traffic and the sounds in her head. Madelyn was elsewhere, not feeling her usual quick-witted self.

Then at the traffic light on the corner of Beverly Glen, Madelyn was surprised to find herself standing immediately offstage as she heard Johnny Carson come back from the commercial break and begin her introduction. She had checked her image in the mirrored green room, completed her vocal warmups and was feeling that welcome familiar flutter of excitement before going on. Her final moments of preparation were interrupted by a sharp pain in her upper right arm. She turned to see her first husband Sam, an angry, almost crazed look on his face. Why had he left the green room? Why hadn't he just stayed home?

"You bitch. You think everybody loves you. I'm the only one you love, though, right, bitch? Right? You're not so wonderful. Not everybody loves you. Don't you forget it."

He loosened his grip long enough for her to escape, through the opening in the curtain into the bright lights of the set where Johnny was waiting, smiling and applauding. She heard the band play her intro, walked over to her marks, and comfortably eased into her practiced show biz persona. The warm applause was an aphrodisiac like no other. She started the verse to "Say It With Music," a song audiences expected to hear from her.

Music is a language lovers understand
Melody and romance wander hand in hand

The irony of the words did not escape her. She hoped the chasm between the airy and romantic lyrics and the realities of her brutal marriage did not show on her face. It was that night when the painful dichotomy of the illusion had almost interrupted her professional demeanor. Was it the awareness of the event nearly 40 years ago that had traumatized her? Or could it have been another time where she had come home from a gig to find him drunk, lying in wait for her? He had beaten her, torn up her arrangements, shredded her life, really.

The traffic was lurching along again, jolting her back into the present.

"I probably should have done this long ago," Madelyn said.

Helen kept her eyes on the road. "I've never been. Hard to imagine you lying on a couch for very long."

Madelyn laughed. Not that it was funny. Just as she peered through the windows of the blue Honda next to her, she sucked in her stomach and felt the impact, crushed under that guy who had burst into her hotel room. Where had that been? Wenatchee? Salem? They never caught him. Why wouldn't these pictures go away? She didn't cancel her show the next night, though. She always went on, no matter what. That was her training and that was her mantra.

For years, she had thought about seeing a psychologist or psychiatrist, anyone who could help her ream out the crap in her head. But Helen was right. Being a legend is hard work.

A week here, a night there, always on the road. Not a normal life. The only one she had ever known. Perfection was a daily requirement. No time for anything else.

"It shouldn't take long," Madelyn said, reassuring herself. "Just a couple of sessions before we fly up to the Fairmont in San Francisco."

She knew it wouldn't be enough, not by a long shot. She had to unload some of it, just let it out somewhere safe. Helen was a dear - as close to being a friend as she had for decades - but Madelyn had secrets she hadn't told anyone, least of all someone who worked for her. She had come to rely on Helen more as the years went by, as the riptide of age swept her out to sea from time to time. Helen could have been her daughter, if she'd taken the time to have one.

"I'll just do a little shopping while you're in there. We passed a mall a while back. You can call me when you're ready."

Madelyn's stomach growled audibly as Helen pulled into the parking lot and into the one remaining open space. Was this hunger or the start of gastrointestinal panic? The two of them sat quietly for a moment, the car engine purring in wait. Madelyn stared at the dashboard. Now she was at the top of the long stairway center stage, her tightly corseted figure dazzling in that long sparkling red dress. The audience started its tumultuous applause before she sang a single note. She looked down to see the waiters smiling and singing as they formed a line at the bottom of the staircase.

Hello, Dolly.

Well, Hello, Dolly

She surely knew how to marshal that luminescence. She loved that moment. She felt transcendent, above all the detritus of real life. Sometimes it was comforting to have that ready-made inspiration on tap, people she had portrayed, inhabited, become if only for a few hours. It was like having a DVD playing inside her head with all the characters on call, like multiple personality disorder without the craziness. If she could only bring it under control.

"OK. I'll see you later, Helen. Don't worry about me. I'll be fine."

She was ready now. Still, this wasn't a performance with memorized, internalized song lyrics - not a script with a role she had under her belt. This was all ad lib, coming from a place completely foreign to her. Her worst nightmare, in a way, like going on stage and not knowing her lines. Or like forgetting those song lyrics the other night at the Bowl - and the other nights. The horror of those moments used to happen in the middle of the night. That was bad enough.

The wall directory was easy to decipher, if only her eyes would focus. "Deidre Collins, Ph.D. Suite 305." After a preventative stop at the restroom, she found the door and cautiously opened it.

Won't someone hear my plea
And take a chance with me

The room was sparsely furnished with six Eames chair knockoffs in various colors. There was a Danish modern coffee table with frayed magazines piled on top. Nondescript art decorated the walls. No one was there. For a moment, she worried she had come at the wrong time. She sat on the green Eames, pulled out her reading glasses, picked up an old magazine and flipped through its pages without comprehending any of it.

The inside door opened quietly, but it was enough to cause Madelyn to drop her magazine to the floor. She awkwardly reached to pick it up and heard a warm, lilting voice.

"Hello. You must be Madelyn Mercer. I'm Dr. Deidre Collins. Please come in." Madelyn followed her down the hall to a well-appointed office. She looked around for the proverbial couch but there wasn't one there. Well, at least, not the kind she had seen in comic strips and in movies. This was more like a living room, with a sofa, two comfortable upholstered chairs, a coffee table, better art on the walls. Her eye caught the Kleenex box on the table, and she felt a grain of gratitude. Why was she so nervous? Her hands felt clammy. She hoped the doctor hadn't noticed that.

"What brings you here today?" Deidre's manner was friendly, if professional. Her face had non-judgmentalness written all over it, a sort of expectant half-smile fixed in place. Her head was slightly tilted to the left, in open anticipation of what Madelyn might say.

Madelyn looked up from her lap and at her dark brown, caring eyes for the first time. For an instant, she was distracted by the beige Chanel suit and the matching Manolo Blahnik shoes. The hair was perfectly styled, not too much makeup, artfully done. It could have been a younger version of herself, if she had gone to college.

"I'm a performer," she began, not knowing how much to say.

"Mmm. Uh huh."

"That's what I do. That's who I am." She had to fight an urge to launch into her opening song from her Kansas City show.

They go wild, simply wild over me
They go mad, just as made as they can be

She knew she had to unpack her trunk of tricks, like how to hold people off, how to avoid any real intimacy, even with poor eager-to-please Helen, her factotum for three decades. It could all start here. Maybe.

"I've heard and seen your name, of course. But I've never seen you perform."

That felt like a sucker punch. She lived in a hermetic bubble in which everyone in it agreed she was a legend, that everyone had heard her voice or seen her on TV or on stage, that everyone thought she was the best ever. She thrust her chin upward a bit to protect against the inadvertent assault, the hurt.

"I've been around a long time. Started when I was nine."

"Why don't you tell me why you're here. How can I help?"

Madelyn sat back, nestling herself into the soft cushions and stumbled on to the darkened stage in her head.

"That's the problem. All I do is perform. A lot has happened and…"

At each word, she reconsidered trusting her. It wasn't about the shrink, really. Madelyn didn't trust anyone and for good reason. The bus of betrayal seemed to stop at every corner.

"You're always on stage, one way or another. Is that right?"

Why had she waited so long to do this? Did she dare hope, and for what?

Now, dearie, don't be late

I want to be there when the band starts playin.'

The band was always playing. That was the problem. What happens if it's gone? Who would she be then?

"Yeah. I am. Always on."

"Even here?"

Whoa. The truth and so soon.

"I don't want to be…on stage here. I've been doing this long enough." She could feel a tear starting to well up in her right eye and immediately grabbed for the convenient box of Kleenex.

Deidre nodded. "It's easy to get caught up in what seems to be, rather than what is. Yes?"

Madelyn shifted in her chair. "I don't know what is. I mean, I know what happened to me. Believe me, I know about all that. But something different is happening now. Worse."

"I want to hear about that when you're ready to tell me. How have you typically handled the crises in your life before this?"

Madelyn smiled at Deidre, meeting her eyes. "I'd cram it all into a performance. Reviewers say I really get under the lyric. No kidding! And now, there's…I don't how to describe it… interference when I'm on stage. Sometimes even when I'm not."

"What do you think will happen here – in this room?" Again, that expectant look that was now inviting.

"I'm afraid I'll lose my…what?…edge? Talent? My voice? Myself." She was stopped at hearing her last word. Lose herself? Is that what's happening?

"Most people gain more in psychotherapy than they lose. It can be scary sometimes, I know. But if you're willing to work with me, we'll need to meet twice a week for a while. Change takes time. Can you do that?"

A tsunami of disappointment swept over her. How could she rearrange her life just like that? There were engagements, obligations…expectations. Fears.

Come Fly with Me

She knew what she needed to do. She was 82, not nearly ready to retire, afraid to think about it. But if she took some time off, nobody would need know the reason for it. There was a gap after this LA gig. At least, they could get started with this excavation, or whatever it would turn out to be. There was something calming about Deidre's style and demeanor. This would be a bumpy road, she knew that, but there was an implied promise of safety about the unknown, perhaps for the first time in her life.

Someone to Watch Over Me

Everything That Mattered

Susannah claimed to have a mystical connection with New York City, unusual for one raised in the brainy bastion of Berkeley, California. She had chosen the city, not only for its performance opportunities, but because it fit her perfectly, better than any of the many other places she had lived. She could breathe here, feel like herself inside its convoluted congestion. Both New York and Susannah were complex organisms, weathering the inevitable, congenital ups and downs without changing their fundamental nature. They had in common a vibrant twitchiness with precarious overtones; but there was also an intrusive darkness, a somber and constant reminder of losses and disappointments.

Pondering the ghostly city in the dead of night, she had forgotten how its reduced tempo renders it quiet, as if at peace with itself. There was only the occasional passing cab or delivery truck. She stood at the window of her 16th floor, rent-controlled apartment on W. 86th Street, a place she had made her own over the years. It was small, as all Manhattan apartments seemed to be to one raised on the West Coast, but it was perfect - just big enough to house her mismatched furniture, her massive, catalogued collection of sheet music, a full keyboard electronic piano and her two Angora cats. When alone, as she almost always was in that sanctuary, she had sometimes mused about the contrast between her compulsive neatness at home and her often disarranged life. She felt in control here. The rest of her life was never quite as malleable.

She was 55 on her last birthday just a few months ago - how did that happen? - and once again, she had to go to her mother to ask for money. If there were other options, she would have taken them, she reassured herself. Her mother extracted the familiar emotional dues for those occasional checks. Susannah knew how the undercurrent inevitably played itself out and what she had to say to navigate through it.

"It's just to tide me over, Mom. The recording contract will be signed this week and Arthur hasn't gotten around to giving me dates yet for the Algonquin. It's coming, though."

"You know, we're up to our asses in medical bills here."

"How's Daddy doing?"

"Not well. Not well at all. I can't get him to take those damned meds. Sometimes he just sits there in his chair all day long, staring. I don't know what to do."

"I know. I'm sorry I can't be there."

"Why don't you just come home, Suz? You could find a nice job in the bookstore just down the road. It would be a regular paycheck. You could stay in your old room. Help out here."

Susannah cringed at the thought and ignored the dismissive tone.

"I'll be home when I can. I will. But now I need a little loan to get through the next month or so."

When she got off the phone, she felt embattled, diminished. She could count on them to come through, at least for the financial support. The emotional part? Never. She assembled her own life, her own self, without help, and in the face of withering criticism and opposition. Multi-layered resentment was the common fuel for all of them living in the musty family home as long as she could remember.

The check had finally come after too many days of anxious waiting. She was certain her mother had delayed it to punish her and at the worst possible time. Susannah believed that if she truly loved her, it would have arrived with dispatch. She didn't need the stress. There had been some bad news. A lot of it.

The first blow came when her agent had called two weeks earlier.

"A European conglomerate is buying Condor Records."

"Oh, OK. Is that good? What does that have to do with me."

"It looks like they're under pressure to trim costs. They're gonna re-release some of your earlier stuff, selecting the best for a compilation. Maybe the last one for a while."

"You mean I'm not going back into the studio?"

"That's right, Suz. I'm so sorry. You know, your last CD didn't sell as well as…"

"I know. I know. It wasn't my fault, Neal. It was the orchestrations. Just way too busy.

I told them that at the time. Nobody would listen and now this happens."

"Yeah. Well. I'm sorry to deliver the bad news. Maybe when the economy picks up again…"

"Yeah…"

"You have a great track record, kiddo. We'll get you signed somewhere else. Just give me a little time."

"But where?"

"I'll take care of it. You're too big in the jazz/cabaret community to go without a record deal."

She trusted Neal, knew he would do his best. Yes, he was right that she had been successful, pretty much on her own.

She had personally sold her CDs in every venue in which she had performed over the past 10-12 years. She enjoyed meeting her fans, chatting them up, hearing their praise. It kept her going. She performed in upscale rooms, almost always to a nearly full house. Critics were mostly kind. She liked it when they compared her unadulterated style to Billie Holiday, when they lauded her well-informed comments about the songs she had chosen, and even more when she brought new interpretations to the songs so many already knew well. Still, the searing criticisms sometimes kept her up at night. Critics would reference her chronic intonation problems, and the fact that she presented herself as a jazz singer but didn't scat. "To be honest," one veteran from a New York newspaper said, "She really can't swing." She didn't much like improvisation, either. Once she got it down, each song would be performed each time exactly the same way. It was her emotional vulnerability that fascinated her audience. No matter the tune, she inserted herself firmly in the middle of every lyric, living it as if were new. And yet, she seemed to slip into the musical cracks as a performer.

Thinking about it now, her whole life had been lived outside the lines of convention. She went to Cal because her parents expected it of her but defiantly majored in Italian literature, hardly a marketable skill. She didn't know what she wanted but she knew she didn't want to be like them. In her junior year, she decided she wanted to write, and so she did. Maybe it was more accurate to say she wanted to live the life of a writer, free and celebrated. No mundane nine-to-five job for her. Her sense of reality often clashed with her romantic notions of how things should be. She had some marginal success, writing first for the school newspaper. One of her short stories was published in a magazine and given a prestigious award. It wasn't enough to make ends meet. Nor did it fulfill her exalted plans for her life.

No one understood her passion for singing. But it was the one thing she could count on for support and even fulfillment. As for the rest, people weren't there for long. Few cared enough to endure her foibles, her temperament. None of the men in her life stayed; once in a while, a casual friendship with a woman. She would refer to herself as a loner. She told herself it was by choice; in truth, it was because Susannah was a difficult person, closed off in many ways. She was hard on people and expected them to focus on her needs, which were prodigious. Her third husband told her she was "aggressively intellectual," which she took as a compliment.

"No one is there," she whispered aloud, as she stood by her apartment window that cold spring night. She turned off the lights so she could see outside more clearly, relieved the sudden darkness didn't disturb the cats, blissfully asleep on the worn blue sofa.

The flame of passion had been ignited quickly, without warning. She had been drinking with friends late one night at an apartment when she overheard a woman singing "I Got A Right to Sing the Blues." Her voice seemed densely laden with the singer's personal experience. The suffering was palpable. She set down her wine glass and walked over to the record player, leaning her ear on the front of the speaker.

"Who is that?" she asked.

"Oh, that's Billie Holiday. A tortured soul. Dead now."

"Dead? Oh, no."

"Yeah, heroin overdose, I think. Not sure. Interesting voice, though, right? Different."

Susannah leaped up and pointed toward the sound.

"That's what I want to do. I want to sing like Billie Holiday."

Everyone laughed. Someone refilled her glass.

"Oh, sure. Everybody wants to do that."

She ignored the joshing, became deadly serious, and stared at the record going around and around.

"No, I think I can do that."

In that providential moment, one song changed the course of her life. That was the road she immediately and urgently felt destined to follow. Impulsively dropping everything else including college and her writer friends, she began to sit in at local clubs, singing for drinks or dinner. She had traveled to Italy to perform, too. Anywhere that would book her. Her quirky, croaky voice was strangely and universally appealing, especially when she added stories about her life to the intimate conversation with her audience.

Susannah smiled, distracted by the sudden movement of the cats behind her, now astir.

"No, you guys. No more for you. You had your dinner." She gazed out the window again. The memories wouldn't stop coming.

The tortuous road to that prized record contract had been filled with travel and with men - lots of men, all of whom lived for her for a while and who helped her along in her career. It wasn't enough. With each ending, she declared they had all let her down. She wasn't a user, she told herself. It was only natural that her closest connections would be with people in that world. Besides, she needed someone to translate her musical requirements to the band. She didn't feel the need to learn music theory or singing technique. The audience response was what mattered. Many of her musicians would grow impatient with her musical laziness and quit, even though they liked her personally. She was a singer with benefits.

Then there had been that other thing. The depression. She remembers it starting in childhood - third grade, she thought.

As an adult, she had started therapy a couple of times. The last shrink had prescribed an antidepressant which she took for a while but stopped because it dried out her throat. There wasn't anything more important than her singing career.

She tried to stay hopeful after the bad news about her CD. When the call came from Arthur, well, it felt like it was all over.

Susannah had an annual gig at the Algonquin, the premier performing room in New York City. She loved doing it each fall, looked forward to it all year. The reviews were almost always good, enlarging her fan base and ensuring gigs in other places. Tourist season was at its peak then, and the booking was a major coup. She thought of herself as a Mabel Mercer, a legendary singer who might perform in one space for decades, maybe into her old age. When Arthur called a week earlier, she assumed he was calling to set the dates. She moved to her desk, sat down and opened her calendar.

"Hello, Arthur. Good to hear from you."

"Susannah, dear, we're going to bring in some new, young talent this fall."

"That's great, Arthur. I can work around that. Maybe I can mentor them. Glad to help."

"Ah, no. The tourists that time of year want to see…new faces. How about we schedule you for a few weeks in the summer instead? I can book you into the entire month of July."

"The summer? When no one's around?"

"I'm sorry, Susannah. That's the best I can do right now. You're a valuable asset to us and we want you back. In the summer."

"No. No. No, I won't do that. Arthur, we've been together for over ten years. I've brought in good business. You owe me. You can't do this."

"I'm sorry. Really, I am. Let me know if your situation changes. We'd love to have you back in July. Let me know as soon as you can."

She admitted she had been difficult at times. That is an affliction all artists share. A year or so before, she had stopped her show only minutes into it because the temperature in the room was too warm and the lights weren't right. They had argued on occasion about salary, too. She liked Arthur even though it was strictly business. Apparently, it was for him, too. Nothing personal. Was it ever otherwise? The reality of it increased her cynicism. She could never go backwards. July? An insult. Absolutely not.

After the call, she sat in her apartment for two days, getting up only to feed the cats. She couldn't understand why this was happening to her. She was smart, talented and successful. Everyone said so. Even in her youthful prime, she was not what people might call pretty. Still, she did what she did well. Well enough, at least. For years.

When she ran out of tears, she agreed to meet a woman friend for lunch, hoping to extract herself from the depths. Annie had known her since Susannah had dropped out of college and gone to Italy to "experience life." Though they met only occasionally, they had no secrets. Susannah told her about the disastrous setbacks, of course, and how she was struggling emotionally. It was Annie who only last year had physically taken her to her own psychiatrist, hoping she could help her good friend.

"Why don't you go back to Melanie? You liked her."

"I tried but she wouldn't see me. Said I called her too often in the middle of the night. Who else should I call? She referred me to somebody else. Right. Start over? I don't think so. That pissed me off, to tell you the truth. And I won't take those damned pills. They made me feel strange and messed up my singing big time. Didn't help, either."

"I understand. Come on. You're not gigging now, right? Did you fill the prescription? Do you still have it?"

"Yeah, I think the bottle is on the counter in the bathroom. Unopened."

"Do it for me. Just for a couple of weeks. Maybe it'll turn you around so you can plan your next triumph. The world awaits!"

Susannah smiled and nodded, and they parted company. She liked Annie but no one could understand the anguish she was feeling. She began to plan, all right, just not what Annie had intended.

It was all too much and had been for a long time. It felt like a struggle to gain an inch of space from the sadness. She could feel her personal tempo slowing, a response to relationships gone bad, the lost career opportunities, the onset of aging. She could put on a brave face for her friends and especially for her audiences. It was so much work. There didn't seem to be a solution. Her career, her identity, her life - all in the toilet.

Three days earlier, she had painstakingly crafted a handwritten note to Annie, thanking her for her support and her friendship. She asked for her forgiveness, knowing her decision would bring grief to her good friend. There would be no note to her hypercritical mother, however. Susannah imagined she would be glad to be rid of her inept, rebellious daughter. There was never any energy to confront her and she certainly wouldn't do it now. She wouldn't blame her mother for ridiculing her talent, her dreams and even her appearance. Not at this point. Too late. It wasn't about others' expectations now. Susannah had outgrown her life. Used herself up. All roads out were blocked or unpalatable. Somewhere in the struggle to stay afloat, she had lost herself.

For those three days, she stayed planted on the couch, reading her old writings. Some of the college stuff wasn't bad, she thought. It brought her momentarily back to the person she once felt herself to be – creative, alive, curious, adventurous. That was another Susannah, another world. What happened to her? It had slipped away. Forever. Was it really ever there? Had she sabotaged herself? It didn't matter. It was almost time. This would be the day.

True to her nature, she had taken the time to pay her bills and pick up her clothes from the cleaners around the corner. If nothing else, she had a strong sense of organization, a compulsive planner. It was essential that everything had been completed. No unfinished business.

She walked over to the occupied cat tree and lovingly stroked the long fur of each one.

"I'll always love you guys. You'll be fine. Don't worry." She moved to her desk and pulled out a Post-It note. She printed her message in a bold hand, in ink.

"There are two cats in apartment 16B. Please take care of them." She folded the paper and placed it in her shirt pocket, included her apartment key, then securely buttoned the pocket flap. There were no tears, no hesitation, no other options.

She opened the window that overlooked the deserted W. 86th Street, smiling for an instant at how clever she had been to ask the super last week to wax the frame so it would glide smoothly. She looked forward to the cool breeze that would propel her quickly to the ground and briefly considered how it would make a poignant New York metaphor. She took a deep breath and, in an instant, the window frame was empty.

Ethel

As soon as she entered any room, Ethel Barrymore left little doubt she was royalty, or at least, its show business equivalent. That square jaw, the penetrating eyes, the erect carriage majestically leading the way. When she spoke, her sculpted, cultivated alto announced this was someone who would not tolerate any trifling.

"Come on, old girl." She looked at the wrinkled face in the mirror. "Don't let those morons get to you."

Today was her big scene with Frank Sinatra in what she suspected might be her final public appearance. She decided that playing a lovable matriarch would be an excellent and memorable way to end it. She had rehearsed for several days with Lettie, her aide, just to be sure she would be letter-perfect, as usual.

She couldn't remember a time when she wasn't famous. Given the rich Barrymore and Drew family legacies - generations of professional actors - she never had a choice. Fortunately, she loved the work, soaked up the adulation, and treasured the elite society in which she fit so seamlessly.

It would be decades before she would admit, and only to close friends, that she and the austere Winston Churchill had been an item; in fact, he had proposed to her more than once. Each time, she denied him, afraid it would hamper pursuit of her real passion, the theater. When she saw his wedding photo on the society page, she found herself both amused and flattered that the new bride bore a striking resemblance to Ethel, herself.

Reminiscing inevitably generated a buoyant mood. Still, Ethel never thought she got the credit she deserved, burdened as she was by comparisons with her two siblings, each with a lesser degree of fame. Jack was flamboyant and arguably the most talented of the three, but he dissolved his gifts in alcohol and suffered a dissolute death at 60. She seldom discussed Jack with interviewers, but when his alcoholism came up, she would claim him to be a victim of family genetics. She missed him every day. In a distant third place in the sub rosa family competition, Lionel signed with MGM, playing secondary but memorable character roles. Since childhood, the boys tacitly accepted Ethel to be the rock, someone they could count on when times were tough. She was the one with the common sense, the problem-solver, and later, the family benefactor.

Ethel was a star, even in those first backyard performances in Philadelphia. When she decided they should do "Camille," she practiced coughing until her parents thought she was actually ill. Her brothers always played supporting roles to her lead, an abiding template for the rest of her life. If asked, she would admit that she liked her men weak and her women interesting.

She wore her storied reputation like a suit of armor, implicitly daring anyone to penetrate the thick metallic coating. If someone were presumptuous enough to approach unbidden, she had only to flash those laser eyes or blow them away with a cryptic verbal body slam. Even at a young age, critics commented on the strength and fullness of her voice. It served her well all those years, where she predictably dominated every performance.

Now, she was playing the acerbic but serene Aunt Jessie, in support of two bigger stars. She was fond of Jessie, perhaps because it was an idealized version of herself. The script had her say, "I'm the 'you can't-hide-a-thing-from-me' kind of aunt." No-nonsense, noble but humble, witty without cruelty. It's as if the part had been written for her by a kindly public relations person.

Though the interview requests had ebbed, there were still some who remembered her from her dazzling stage performances. Critics from another generation had called her the "Washington Monument of the Theater," the "Grand Dame," and other fawning approbations. In recent years as good parts eluded her, she had deigned to act in the flickers, which paid far better than the stage. Motion pictures were considered an art form by many, but Ethel thought it an ephemeral amusement at best - the cotton candy of gourmet food. People came and went so quickly, their reputation created by a studio flack, not by virtue of any talent. And so, with great reluctance, she had signed the contract to play Aunt Jessie in the Warner Bros. musical, "Young at Heart." It was 1954 and she would soon be 75 years old. She was struggling.

At her peak, she could read a script once and have it down, but those days had evanesced. She and Lettie worked for hours until Ethel could respond as Aunt Jessie, picking up each cue without hesitation. Her dressing room on the Warners lot was capacious by Broadway standards, but she knew her co-stars had nicer ones. Both Frank Sinatra and Doris Day were at the top of the popularity charts in both music and movies. Their names above the title would guarantee box office success. Billed as a supporting player, Ethel feigned indifference to what she considered a professional snub.

"You know, Miss Barrymore," Lettie reassured her, "neither of them has your talent or experience. Or, your, what do the critics call it, charisma."

She fidgeted with the script sitting on her dressing room table while Lettie went to the set to determine when Ethel would be needed. Everyone knew Sinatra tolerated only one take before losing focus, so filming her few scenes with him had to be accomplished perfectly the first time. The assistant director stood in for Frank during the tedious rehearsals.

Ethel genuinely liked other performers and was seldom jealous, confident in her own unique talent. The one thing she would not tolerate was unprofessionalism. She respected her craft too much to endure pretenders. That's how she thought of Frankie, whom she called "the boy crooner," an egotist who thought he was above working on a scene with his fellow actors. No one labored as hard as she had, and as she still did, for that matter. During their business lunch, her agent mentioned that Sinatra had demanded that the ending of the film be changed so his character wouldn't die. Sinatra reminded her of some of the arrogant stage actors she had to appear with in New York. They all thought they were gods, too.

There was a soft knock on the door.

"Miss Barrymore. You're wanted on the set, whenever you're ready."

She liked the AD. He was deferential and polite, knew his place.

Lettie came in after him.

"Miss Barrymore, are you ready? If not, I can get them to postpone. But Mr. Sinatra is waiting."

"Oh, he is, is he?" She took one last look in the mirror, smoothed her housedress and allowed Lettie to touch up her hair a bit. "All right. We mustn't keep Mr. Sinatra waiting, must we?"

Ethel was discomfited that she was forced to use a wheel-chair to get around. It was painfully reminiscent of Lionel's pathetic last years as he was losing his faculties. Still, it made it easier for her to husband her strength, and to navigate around the set between scenes. No one in the movie audience would know how fragile she was these days.

The set was bustling with activity, everyone in simultaneous motion. This would be the first part of the scene where Aunt Jessie enters the family's living room to find Sinatra's character, a stranger to the family, sitting at the piano. She had tried it several ways at home. Should she be surprised? Frightened? Nonchalant? Challenging? There were so many options and the director, Gordon Douglas, had left her on her own. After all, who could instruct her in the art of playing a scene?

Lettie helped her to her feet.

"I've got you, Miss Barrymore. Don't you worry."

"I'm OK. Lettie. Please let go. Goodness gracious. I'm fine."

Sinatra smiled and nodded at her from the piano bench as she found her mark. She looked back at him with her practiced grandeur and steely brown eyes, just the slightest upturn at one corner of her mouth. There was something about the bright lights, a touchstone, a reminder that people wanted her, worshipped her. The adrenalin rise would soon be followed by an inevitable calmness. She was in her element. It was all so easy, if only she could walk without a limp and remember her lines.

Under her breath, she muttered, "Let's get on with it. Movies. Not like the theater."

She continued to stand while the costume, makeup and hair people fussed over her. She could feel her knees quivering and knew her standing position would be possible for a few more minutes, at best. To distract herself, she transported her thoughts to the old Booth Theater, during the early part of the century when there were still foot-candles burning downstage. So comforting to bring back the acrid aroma of the gas and the dense smell of greasepaint. The odors of a Hollywood soundstage were resistant to characterization, not nearly as charming or emotionally evocative. There was too much noise and confusion. One had to focus, push away everything else. In those seconds, she had to become Aunt Jessie, the no-nonsense but warm helpmate.

In real life, the "warm" part was sometimes obscured within the fortress of her professional demeanor. A star had to remain a bit aloof, detached from those around her, to preserve the sense of awe she so deftly evoked in others. Chit-chatting with others was draining, especially when preparing to go on. These people were definitely not dinner-guest material. She needed to concentrate, silently go over her lines. She tried to conjure up a light moment from her past to get into the scene.

"Ready, Mr. Sinatra? Miss Barrymore?"

Straighten up, she told herself. Speak from the diaphragm. Make those eyes twinkle.

"Yes, Gordon."

"Come on, Ethel. Let's do this." She didn't need Sinatra's flippant encouragement. Nor did she appreciate his familiarity.

She watched Sinatra lean over the piano, heard the playback music begin and waited for her cue. Deep breath. She took a few hesitant steps in and started to say her first line.

"Cut! Miss Barrymore. Remember, we need you to take a few more steps toward Frank before you begin your line. Again, please."

She felt her face flush and hoped no one had noticed. "All right. Yes. Of course." She thought she saw a look of impatience cross Sinatra's face.

"Action!"

She propelled herself into the living room, stopped at the piano, and spoke her line.

"For all I know, you could be a burglar, planning to make off with the piano. I don't know who you are but I'm Jessie. Aunt Jessie, just to be perfectly clear."

"Ah, of course. The name fits the room. Chintz curtains, doilies on the table."

"The name came first, chintz afterwards."

"Cut!" Miss Barrymore, the line is, 'The name came first, doilies after.' Let's go again."

Damn. She spoke the line to herself. "The name came first, doilies after." OK. Got it. She was embarrassed, unfamiliar with professional frailty. With considerable effort, she willed her body back to the starting point. She glared at Sinatra and did the scene again, this time perfectly.

"Cut! Great job, everybody. That's a print. Take an hour while we set up the next shot. Miss Barrymore, we'll give you plenty of notice."

"Thank you, Gordon."

"Nice goin', Ethel."

Why did Frankie have to comment on everything? It's pathetic that he feels compelled to seize the focus. She forced out a faint smile.

Lettie quickly stepped in to help Ethel back to the wheelchair.

"You were wonderful, Miss Barrymore."

"Yes, Lettie. Thank you."

She knew she'd be tired and was relieved that the takes and the scenes were short. Did Gordon know of her limitations? Could anyone see her struggle? The stamina wasn't there anymore, unpredictable and elusive. Last week, however, she was able to talk on the phone for over an hour with Tallulah

Bankhead, and felt marvelous afterwards. Now she needed to return to her dressing room to have a cup of tea and maybe take a nap.

She was still catching her breath when Lettie poured the hot English blend into the antique cup that went everywhere with them. She knew she could count on the demure, overweight woman, whom she had hired years ago in New York.

"Lettie, could you find me a tea cake or two? I think I'm hypoglycemic. Even a little candy would be fine. And before I forget, would you please call Mrs. Roosevelt and postpone our dinner until tomorrow? I'm going to be unavailable tonight, I'm afraid."

"Of course, Miss Barrymore. Miss Hepburn asked if you might be available for a dinner party with Mr. Cukor on Saturday."

"I hope you're speaking of Kate, not that unfortunate urchin, Audrey. I like Kate so much. Smart, funny, a clever woman. If my schedule is clear, tell her yes. Her parties are so stimulating, with cultured people at the table."

"I'll take care of it, Miss Barrymore."

She dearly loved people who amused and stimulated her, especially those who weren't after something. Family relationships hadn't worked out so well, but she maintained a strong core of friendships, many of them for decades. All of them were famous.

Her thoughts often wafted back to Jack, in spite of his lack of discipline and the relentless chaos in his life, but she had unfinished business with older brother Lionel, especially when the topic of politics arose. When he announced his support for Thomas Dewey over FDR, she glibly and publicly described Dewey as "the bridegroom on a wedding cake," words gleefully picked up by the media. It became sufficiently contentious between them that she stopped invited him to dinner. Poor Lionel. She was lost in grief when Jack died, but she doubted she would feel much when Lionel finally went. Never the same with him. When she thought of those early years with Jack, the pleasant memories helped assuage her residual guilt. Could she have done more to help him? Reverie about her siblings easily crept into her daily existence, especially when she was working. In many ways, she was still one of the three Barrymores.

This whole movie stop-and-go business was irritating and exhausting. She never did understand how Lionel stood it all those years. MGM was little more than a factory. All the studios were. No wonder Jack drank himself to death. "The Great Profile" could no longer recite Shakespeare, so the movies with its short scenes was all he could manage.

She was aware, and only a little dispirited that this could be her swan song, that the mighty engine was running out of steam. She didn't belong in this business anymore. Sitting at the dressing table, she slumped in her wheelchair. She was bone-tired and at that moment, regretted agreeing to play this part.

Ethel glanced up at the sepia Shubert playbills taped to her mirror. She wasn't one to keep scrapbooks or souvenirs of her many triumphs and forgot why she held on to these. Perhaps it was Lettie's doing. No matter what, Jack's picture would have a prominent place on her dressing room mirror; she had not left that to chance, reminding Lettie whenever they moved to a new theater.

"He was so very handsome, wasn't he, Miss Barrymore?"

"Yes, he certainly was. Gentle, kind. If a bit bohemian."

"I wish I had seen him onstage."

"When he was sober, he was the best there was. But…"

Her voice trailed off, leaving Lettie in silence.

She had retired once before, back in 1936, announcing to the press that she would devote the rest of her life to mothering her three children. It didn't work out as she had hoped. A year later, she was back on Broadway in another smash. Now the children were grown and gone, except dear Sammy who took care of things at home. She seldom thought about the marriage to Russell and when she did, she couldn't remember why she did it. It was expected, certainly, and helped stave off the stage-door Johnnies - and any whispered gossip involving her female friends. Old maids were unseemly. But Russell turned out to be a bounder and when he got some young trollop pregnant, Ethel divorced him. The public hadn't known it, but she had filed for divorce several times before, each time dissuaded by the ironclad prohibitions of her Catholic faith. and perhaps her own guilt about being pregnant before the wedding. But the little bastard kid was too much. In retrospect, marriage and motherhood were very much like stage credits, giving her persona greater resonance. She realized she had been badly cast in both roles.

She sat, drinking her tea, gazing into the mirror. Lettie broke the silence.

"Here are some cookies. They're shortbread, your favorite. Can I bring you anything else?"

"No. That'll do. Thank you."

Lettie had learned the skill of entering and leaving without raising any dust. When she wasn't performing her duties, she was nearly invisible.

More often these days, Ethel's thoughts flowed backwards, to those intoxicating days when she was the toast of Broadway, the life of any party, the object of male and female attention. At this point, she longed to make it through this film without further problems. Really, though, what she most anticipated was dinner with Eleanor tomorrow night. They would talk politics and reminisce.

Lettie tapped lightly on the door, thinking her boss was likely napping. She found her gazing into the mirror.

"Miss Barrymore, Mr. Douglas said you won't be needed anymore today and that he looks forward to seeing you again tomorrow. He hopes to wrap your scenes by lunch time."

"Oh, good. I'm tired. There's nothing like one's own bed, is there?"

"Let me help you to the car."

"Thank you, dear. You're a jewel. I'm ready to go home."

It was almost over.

Gerry's Interview

Some days, it's hard for me to remember why I'm here. I know where I am. I'm here at Emerald Glen. I mean at this point in my life. First off, I need to tell you I never wanted to be a movie star. Momma drove me to my dancing and singing lessons. Picked me up right after school. She kept telling me how wonderful I was, how I was making her so proud. Nobody in Beatrice, Nebraska had ever been in movies, so I don't know why she thought it would be me up there on the big screen. Oh, I had done community theater, church socials, you know. Typical small-town stuff. Big frog and all that.

I don't know why you wanted this interview, to tell you the truth. It all happened a long time ago. It's nice to be remembered, though. Memory's a funny thing, isn't it?

I know it was spring when we left because of the smell of the white blossoms on the pear tree in the front yard. Daddy was waving goodbye and Momma was crying in the car. They never fought about anything, so I guess they thought this was the right thing to do. Him staying home, I mean. I'd graduated from high school the day before. Going to Hollywood was a big improvement over working in Studd's Western Wear, I'll tell you.

Momma found us a—what was it?—oh, yeah, a furnished apartment right away. It was a lot smaller than our house in

Nebraska. The neighborhood was a little dicey. I was nervous about everything but, boy, she was enthusiastic enough for both of us. She took me to auditions for night clubs, if you can believe that. She lied about my age and I got hired pretty quick. I guess I looked older. Momma kept telling me not to be scared, that when men would try naughty things, I should just smile and say, "No, thank you, sir." I understood that but it was a lot harder when I met the owner of this club—Mr. Tony Chandler, himself. What year would that have been? Let's see. I was 17, right out of high school, so it would have been…let me think…I was born in 1920. So, 17! Yes, 17.

Of course, I already knew who Mr. Chandler was. We listened to his records all the time at home. Didn't you love "I Remember Spring"? He was on the radio, too. My mother adored him. So the thought I was singing in his night club made everything a huge, glamorous adventure. Movie stars came into the club all the time and requested songs. When Mr. Chandler walked in, I tell you, the Red Sea parted, and everything sparkled. He was charismatic and so handsome. Shorter than I had thought. Well, I was short, too, so I guess he liked that I made him look taller. I loved it when he came in and asked me to sing his big hits Then, on my nights off, he would take me to dinner at some fancy place and we'd go back to his huge mansion to, um, watch movies. You know.

I can't tell you how I got to Paramount. I made a lot of movies there, all small parts. Later, I found out Mr. Chandler owned part of the studio. By then, I had an agent. Bernie Morgan was his name. To get me a part, Bernie told a guy in the front office that I could ride a horse. Well, I'll tell you, that weekend, he had me out in Griffith Park, teaching me how to do it. By then, I'd learned that Hollywood was all about illusion. Not everyone was as nice as Mr. Chandler. I don't want to talk about that part.

I think it's almost time for lunch. Or dinner. We'll have to stop soon.

You know, I wanted to be a reporter just like you. Momma thought I belonged on the stage. She was probably right. She usually was. I played one in a movie once.

Anyway, all my life I was told I was cute and perky, sort of America's Sweetheart, you know? But those people at Paramount said my hair was too dark, my bosom too small and that I needed help with makeup. Everything about me was wrong. I went shopping with a girlfriend and bought clothes I thought the studio would approve of. I still have most of them. What was her name? She was sleeping with the production manager. It was so long ago, wasn't it?

It was like I was on a treadmill, one movie after the other. I can't remember all the names, but a lot of them involved horses. And then, wow, I was cast in a film with Johnny McBride. It was called "Frontier Gentleman." Johnny was a big star, so I figured this small-town girl had made good. Over the next few years, we did a bunch of pictures together. I was the trusting, clueless wife who needed rescuing in the last reel. I didn't mind because it was all so much fun. Johnny was very sweet to me so when I heard he'd been murdered…Oh, wait. I'm forgetting some things here. Sorry. That happens a lot these days. Now, where was I? What was your question?

Oh, yeah. Remember Fred Astaire and Ginger Rogers? Weren't they wonderful? They made a bunch of pictures together at RKO. Sometimes years would pass between them. Well, that's what happened with me and Johnny. OK, I did have a big crush on Johnny. Who didn't? He was tall, well-built, didn't drink too much. So many people did back then. We spent a lot of time together off-screen, but you don't have to know about that. It was his eyes, I think. The way he looked at me. I'd just melt. They were much softer when we were together than they were on the screen. He was so...I don't know.

When the westerns stopped, I fell back into small parts. Even did a little TV when that came along. One afternoon—I think it was around three o'clock—I got a call from Bernie who told me the western movies I made with Johnny were being adapted into a weekly television series for NBC. Johnny and I would be back together again. Between you and me, I worried a little. I was older, you know, not a dewy-eyed ingenue. It was the 1950s. "Ozzie and Harriet," "Father Knows Best," and all that. At that time, though, westerns were very big. They're not now.

I don't know why you want to hear about all this. I do want to say that all this was really taking its toll on me. The Hollywood life, the long hours. Momma died, which was really hard. My marriage had ended. I had a couple of good friends and that was my life. Period! So much going on. It all ran together. No, I don't want to talk about that crappy marriage to what's his name. Talk about illusion. He had neglected to tell me he had a boyfriend in Santa Barbara. Anyway, it didn't last long, and I moved on. Marriage came second to my career, to tell you the truth. So, I asked myself, why not do a television series? It was something to pass the time and pay the bills.

When the script was finally delivered, Bernie was upset because my part was so small. I didn't have many lines in all those movies, either, so I don't know what he expected. It was OK with me. Really, it was. Even after it aired, I could still go to the market and not be—what's the word?—uh, recognized most of the time. Johnny and I sort of picked up where we left off. There wasn't a lot of private time, if you know what I mean, but enough. At least for me.

Damned if that low-budget little series didn't go on and on and on. Oh, pardon my French. I think it ran for seven years.

Funny, huh? It was terrific to get a regular paycheck. I tried to be smart with the money. Bought a cute little cottage in the Santa Monica canyon. Traveled some, went to visit my cousins in Nebraska. To them, I was a big celebrity. That was fun.

After a while, I could see the savings dwindling down, but I didn't know how to stop it. I had heard all those horror stories about getting ripped off by managers, so I never trusted anyone with my money.

Wait. Give me a second. I'm trying to stay on track here. Where was I? Oh yeah. Johnny. I got that awful phone call in the middle of the night. When the phone rings at that hour, it's never good. I still get the willies when I think about it. I don't remember how Bernie told me, his exact words, but he said Johnny was dead. That he had shot himself. I didn't see Johnny much after the series was canceled. We met once in a while for dinner, you know. I knew he had been sleeping with the wife of some big movie executive. Johnny told me the husband was "connected" and could bump anyone off he wanted. But then he met someone else, a rich widow. Woo-hoo. That was OK with me. That part of our relationship had ended years before. Well, more or less. Johnny won't like it if I talk about that.

The newspapers said it was suicide. I don't believe it. Johnny was a happy-go-lucky guy. Yeah, he was between pictures, but he talked about this new woman all the time. He was really wildly in love with her. I wondered how the wife took the whole thing. Johnny said she was crazy jealous and that they had fought a lot when they were together. It's hard to think a woman would slug a guy, especially someone as big as Johnny but she did. No wonder he cut it off. I bet she had him killed because he was seeing this other woman. Then it occurred to me, was I next? I was scared shitless. Excuse the language. After all, we saw each other almost to the end. Now and then, I mean. Did she know? Oh my God. Was she crazy enough to come after me?

I locked all the doors in my house and didn't even answer the phone for a long time. At night, I'd turn on the TV so anyone wandering around outside could hear someone was here and wouldn't break in. I know, I know. That was stupid. Anyone who wanted to kill me wanted me to be here. But you know. I was out of my mind with fear. I could picture Johnny's face when I'd close my eyes, imagining his head being blown off by some thug with a five o'clock shadow in a dark suit. Sort of like George Raft, you know?

I don't know how many days and hours passed. One afternoon, someone knocked on my door and I almost jumped through the roof. When I looked out the peephole, I saw Sandra, my friend from down the road so I let her in. Isn't it funny how I can bring back how terribly scared I was, but I can't remember much about those years we did "Frontier Gentleman"? That show went on a lot longer than my fear did. The mind's a funny thing, don't you think?

You know, I don't think they ever did solve the case. The police called it a suicide and let it go at that. Those big studio guys controlled everything in those days. When time passed by and I wasn't murdered, I started to relax. Maybe I was low enough on the hit list that she wouldn't bother with me. I think she's dead now. I hope so. I think about Johnny almost every day.

Don't know if I told you this but one night, he came to me in a dream. He said very firmly, "Gerry, you need to start your life over again. You have to get out of the movies. You're never going to be a star. It'll kill you."

It was funny he would tell me that because I never wanted to be a movie star. It was all sort of an accident. One day became another and there I was, singing for Tony Chandler in his night club. Did I tell you that story? If I didn't, remind me later. Did he say "it" will kill me or "she" will kill me? Anyway, I needed to do something to get out of the house, get my mind off it.

I believe there's a reason for everything. If Johnny warned me to get out of the business, maybe he was right. The money was running low—fast. I knew I had to do something. I called a friend at Republic Studios I had met at a party a year or so back. You know, one of the good things about this business is that you know everybody one way or another and it's all one big family – except some I could mention. Anyway, I called this guy and asked if he had any jobs open.

He said, "You sure, honey? All I have right now is a slot in the secretarial pool. This isn't the place for you."

I told him I needed the job and that I had taken typing in high school. Even got an A. I promised to practice at home.

Then he told me, "OK, if you're sure."

I wasn't but this is what I needed to do. He asked if I was worried someone there would recognize me. Ha! That was the least of it. Most of my career happened a decade or more before and I was never a star. Never wanted to be. Most of the pictures and even the TV show had me in costume. I didn't think anybody would know who I am or even who I was. Oh. Look. My shoes don't match. Huh. One's just a little browner than the other. Can you see that? I wonder how that happened. Probably that housekeeper mixed them up. She doesn't pay attention to these important details. Yesterday, I walked into the dining room without my shoes. Imagine that!

Now, where was I? Did I tell you about my trip with my mother to California? Wait. I remember now.

People ask me if I was depressed about having to do this. You know, being a secretary. No, not at all. I knew a long time ago that this little actressy thing wouldn't last. Once you get old in Hollywood, you might as well quit. Nobody wants you, anyway. This was something I could do to fill my days and pay the bills. I never really wanted to be a movie star.

Republic was just a small studio, not like the big ones—MGM, Warners or Paramount. I'd been there once before, dubbing one of the westerns, I think. The secretarial pool was on the third floor, all of us in the same room, each with her own little desk and typewriter. Honestly, when I walked in, it looked like a movie set. It seemed oddly familiar. What was the name of the movie with all the women in the same room sitting at typewriters? Wasn't Joan Crawford in it? Maybe it was Joan Blondell.

Anyway, I had a desk by the window so I could watch people walking by on their way to the set. The young kids in the secretarial pool didn't know anything about me and didn't care. They already had their own clique. I think that's what finally got to me. It wasn't the daily grind, typing invoices and correspondence all day. That took my mind off Johnny and everything else. But those dreadful girls snubbed me. They didn't think I could hear them whispering.

Miranda was the head of the department, about ten years older than me and I know she resented my being there. She lorded it over all these young women and flouted her power, demanding they stay late or work through lunch. When she asked me to stay late for some project, the question always had a barb attached.

"Is the movie star available to stay late?"

I always said, "Yes," but it wasn't enough for her.

"I thought you might be going to a big premiere tonight or something."

I'd smile and do what she asked but we didn't like each other much. Even so, I worked there a long time. It paid pretty well, not as much as my acting days, but enough to live on. I loved driving through those studio gates every morning. Took me back, you know?

One afternoon, one of the bosses called me into his office. I was nervous. Oh, no.

Was he going to fire me? Try to seduce me? Worse, was he going to try to get me back into pictures?

He had a deep, gravelly voice. "Mitchell Ellis is looking for someone to answer his fan mail. You know who he is?"

Sure, I knew. He reminded me a bit of Johnny McBride, but he was an honest-to-God movie star. He wasn't just in westerns but in dramas and musicals. He'd been nominated for an Oscar for his role as Thomas Jefferson. Should've won, too. I voted for him. My boss had put in a good word already. The job was mine if I wanted it. Miranda was probably glad to get rid of me.

I hoped the pay was good working for Mr. Ellis. Even if it wasn't, it would be a lot more fun. I knew how to answer fan mail. I still got letters from people from time to time, commenting on the TV show usually, rather than the old movies. It's nice to be remembered. I still get one once in a while here. Nice. Really nice.

Anyway, Mr. Ellis asked me to meet him at his house in, where was it? Somewhere off Sunset. Bel Air? Yes, Bel Air. It was at the top of Bellagio and had a fabulous view of downtown LA. I had been to a lot of Hollywood parties in my time, but this house was something else. A butler answered the door wearing a morning coat. Can you believe it? I was ushered into the largest living room I'd ever seen, way bigger than my house. There was a massive grand piano in the middle and tons of overstuffed, expensive furniture. I just could picture all the parties, the big stars who drank and schmoozed there. When I sat down, I wondered if Clark Gable had perched himself on that leather chair by the window.

When Mr. Ellis entered, he looked exactly as he did on the screen. Big, virile, with an overgrown moustache, and longish hair that curled around his ears. His intense blue eyes were arresting and compelling.

"Nice to meet you, Gerry. I'm Mitchell Ellis."

I laughed out loud, because it was absurd that anyone on the planet would not know who he was.

I stood as tall as I could and told him, "It's an honor to meet you, Mr. Ellis."

"It's Mitch," he said. "And the honor is mine. I enjoyed your pictures with Johnny McBride. And I watched a lot of the TV series, too. You were a good actress."

I remember my exact words. His, too. Isn't that funny? Like watching a movie.

"Thanks. That means a lot, coming from you. No Academy Award nominations on my shelf."

"Not sure there'll be more on mine, either. I know Abe probably told you but I'm getting so much mail now that my staff can't keep up. I need another hand here. Someone who knows the business. Like you."

"I guess that's me. Does this mean I'm hired?"

"Sure, if you want the job. Frankly, I wonder how long you'll last. Another audition will come along eventually, and you'll be gone."

"Nope. No way. I'm done. It's like there's an hourglass and when your time's up…"

I hoped Mitch wouldn't be one of those—what do you call them—egomaniacs who live their lives with one eye on the mirror. I wondered what people would write to really famous movie stars. Over the years, I got some pretty weird mail, like marriage proposals or people claiming to be the child I gave up for adoption. No, I never had a child, if you're asking. Never wanted kids. And I never wanted to be a movie star, either. Life is so funny.

Say, I don't want to take up too much of your time. I know you're busy and need to get on with your day. Are you on a deadline? Before you go, though, I want to say that the job with Mitch was a complete delight. There were several of us answering the mail that came in and, boy, he was right. There was a ton of it. Some of it was sad—one mother begged for money for her son's surgery. That got to me. And some were funny in a peculiar sort of way. Why would anyone want a fingernail clipping? Some woman in Dubuque sure did and even sent a SASE. Mitch and I laughed about that for a long time. He was still big at the box office. I guess his hourglass had more sand in it than mine did.

Anyway, the next time I turned around, I was nearly 60. Thanks to Mitch, I had saved and invested enough so that I no longer had to work. I wanted to. I can't tell you how much I enjoyed pulling up that long driveway each morning. And what do you know? He never made a pass. Not once. Damn it.

People always want to hear about the men. I think some things should remain private, don't you? I didn't want to marry again. It would just complicate things. I went out with friends on weekends. I took a cab when I went out. A few drinks and I could forget my own address! My friends thought it was funny, but I could tell there was a problem. One afternoon, I went to the freezer to get some ice and found my car keys in there. Everybody forgets things when they're 60, don't they?

And then, bingo! Enter stage right. Another act in this funny little life of mine. You sure you want to hear all this? OK.

One day, when we were taking our lunch break, Mitch mentioned an actor friend about my age who had been doing a bunch of nostalgia shows.

I didn't want to pretend I knew, since I hadn't ever heard of such a thing. I had to ask.

Mitch told me it's for movie and TV people who have been out of the public eye for a while. They were once famous but now they sell their autographs. And their 8x10s, if they have them. He said Mickey Rooney does this all the time. And the kid who used to be on 'Lassie.' What was his name? Mitch told me, "You can make good money, Gerry. You'd be surprised how many people remember you. Or would, if they saw an 8x10 from one of your movies, especially the ones with Johnny."

It was like somebody told me the moon was made of Velveeta. I couldn't imagine people paying money for my signature, much less anyone who would want to meet me. Why? I was just somebody's sidekick. It was a long time ago. I never wanted to be a big movie star. And I was sure I didn't want to leave Johnny. I mean Mitch. I loved it there. We were all good friends. It was like being on a set.

I went home that night, made myself a gin and tonic. My old agent, dear Bernie, probably had some leftover 8x10s. And maybe Paramount would have some in the files. I started to talk to myself. What if nobody knows who you are? You'll be sitting at a table all by yourself watching hundreds swarm around Mickey Rooney. I wondered what Johnny would have wanted me to do. Then, I could see his face, smiling down at me with love in his eyes, telling me I should do it. OK, Johnny, if you say so.

I took the morning off and drove down Melrose. I was surprised and a little sad when I found out poor Bernie had died, but the guy who took over his agency had left me a packet of photos. Wow, was that me? I looked so young. Not bad, either, if I do say so. I checked the Thomas Guide and found the publicity office at Paramount. They had tons of stills from our pictures together. When I opened the package, I felt that same jolt of electricity I did when Johnny would come into the room. It would be lovely to help people remember him and talk about what a wonderful actor he was.

That first nostalgia show almost didn't happen. I had trouble finding it, then the parking. Worst of all, I had to talk my way in.

The guy at the door was a snotty, fuzzy-faced punk. "And who are you with?"

I wasn't with anybody. Somebody had set it up. Who, exactly? I couldn't remember.

He called another guy over who waved me in.

When the creep at the door didn't know who I was, my anxiety zoomed. What was I doing here? Who was I kidding?

I pressed my folder of photos under my arm and walked into the room like I belonged, using the demeanor I had learned in the movies. The room was huge, with at least 30-40 tables in rows. I flashed back to the first time I walked into Republic Studios and saw all the secretarial desks positioned like soldiers in a platoon. I moved around the edge of the room so I could see name plates on the desks. The first one I saw said "Whitey Holton." I was excited to see him. He had been Johnny's stunt man, taking those dangerous leaps and falls off mountains and the tops of buildings. His eyes lit up when he saw me.

"Gerry! Gerry! Where have you been? Whatever are you doing here?"

"I wonder that myself." I was so relieved to see a familiar face.

"Uh oh. Is this your first time?"

"I guess I'm a nostalgia show virgin." That made him throw back his head and laugh.

"Let's walk around and find your table." He grabbed my arm and, like the gentleman I remembered him to be, guided me to the other side of the room. It wasn't until I saw the "Geraldine Leonard" name plate that I knew I was truly welcome here. The guy at the next table looked familiar, but then a lot of these people did. I just couldn't place him.

"Hi, Gerry. Gordon Beckett. We did some pictures together." My mind was blank. "You know? "The Scarlet Saddle," and "Wanted for Murder"?

I smiled and nodded, but I had no clue. Did he have the right person? Why is he asking me this? It didn't matter. The doors opened and people filed in. Some were coming my way and I forced what I hoped was a genuine smile. When I saw it was an older woman and a teenage boy, I relaxed. And I can remember the whole scene. So odd.

"You're Geraldine Leonard, aren't you? I was telling my son just the other day about going to see your movies. You were wonderful. So courageous."

"Hello. Thanks so much. Happy to meet you. Thanks for coming." Now what do I say? Oh yeah, the photos.

"Would you like an autographed photo? It's only $25." I picked up my Sharpie, poised for the inscription.

"Oh, I don't think so. Thanks, anyway. But we are both so thrilled to meet you, aren't we, Jonah?"

The kid looked a whole lot less than enthusiastic. There goes my first customer. No sale. Then a creepy, middle-aged guy came up to my table.

"Gerry. Hey. I'm Pete." He shook my hand so hard I thought he might break a bone. "I've seen every movie you made with Johnny McBride. He was such a macho dude. So cool."

Made me wish he were here. He'd know how to do this with more panache. Where are you, Johnny? Why did you go away?

"Ya know, I've been trying to remember the name of the one you guys made, I think it was around 1955, just before the

TV series. It was the one where Johnny was being hunted by his brother who blamed him for their parents' death. Ya know the one I mean?"

It sounded familiar. Maybe. I wasn't sure what to say to him. Out of nowhere, I started to feel funny, almost—what's the word—disoriented. Sort of out of my body. For a minute, I forgot where I was. My ears plugged up. I saw someone standing in front of me. Did I know him? I looked around, trying to figure out where I was and why I was here. I think I signed the photo, collected the money and shook the guy's hand again. There were others who wanted to meet me, and I hoped they wouldn't ask me any questions about my career. As you can see, sometimes I can recall exact dialogue, but other times...I was glad when it was over, and I could go home.

Problems happened when I was going somewhere, too. I'd start off for the grocery store, going to pick up a few items for dinner, you know, and forget which way to turn. I didn't know if I was lost or just forgot how to get there. So I sold my car. It was much easier to call a cab or just take the bus.

Do you think it's time for lunch now? I remember eating breakfast. We had bacon and eggs so it must have been breakfast, right?

Well, there were more shows, I'm happy to tell you. I enjoyed meeting people and was always surprised they knew who I was. Most of their questions were about Johnny so it probably didn't seem strange to them that I didn't know the answers. Those shows made me feel close to Johnny. I made him proud, I know.

Why are you asking about all this, again? I'm sorry, but I've forgotten why you're here. Do you know Johnny? I know where I am. I'm in the assisted living place, aren't I? Being here is like doing the autograph shows where people seem to know me.

The questions are different but most of the time I can answer them. Oh, I know. I hope I've given you a good interview. It has been a long time since I've done this. You're not from *The National Enquirer*, are you?

What did you say your name was, again? I'm Gerry.

THE PLAYS

Life Without

A dark comedy in two acts

The Setting:

A high-rise condo in Century City, well-appointed but not too high-end. The furnishings are contemporary, the usual selection of couch and chairs, tables, lamps. There's a desk in the corner, piled with books and papers, and a laptop. On the desk is an autographed baseball in a little plastic case. There's a TV set in the room, opposite the couch. There's a door to the other rooms via an interior hall stage right, an exterior door to a hallway upstage left. It is early fall in 2005.

The Characters:

(three women, one man)
ROBBIE: She is in her 40s
LAURIE: She is also in her 40s. ROBBIE's domestic partner
STAN: He's a dapper dresser but paunchy and hardly attractive, about 65.
SARAH: She is married to STAN; she's a paraplegic in a wheelchair, about 60.

Act One

SCENE ONE

(All four characters are sitting in the living room, with the remnants of dessert, wines and wine glasses on the table.

STAN

And, of course, she was very grateful for my help. She was very nice to me when I saw her backstage at the awards show at Town Hall. I tell a funny story about her in my new show here in town. It's in two weeks. You'll both come, right?

LAURIE

You're still performing then?

SARAH

He won't… *(starts to say something but he cuts her off)*

STAN

Sarah wants me to stop.

SARAH

I know he'll never give it up. He loves it so much.

STAN

The show will be at the Criterion. When I was in New York, Bob Schuster told me mine was the best show he had seen this year.

LAURIE

Sorry. Who's that?

SARAH

He's the critic for the News-Press. Well, he used to be.

STAN

Julie Salome came to every performance. You know who that is, right? *(everyone nods)* She loved my shows. She always sat in the front row, laughed at all my jokes.

LAURIE

(nods, forces a smile) Mmm hmm.
(ROBBIE is clearly not present in this conversation)

STAN

This season, I'm doing a Cole Porter show. Starts in two weeks. I'm already working on another one. The public demands keep me going. It's not fair to them to stop.

ROBBIE

(almost absent-mindedly) More wine?

LAURIE

Absolutely!
    (she pours all around, nearly wolfs hers down)

ROBBIE

(trying to be polite) What is it you do, Sarah?

STAN

She books my shows, takes the tickets…

ROBBIE

(interrupting) No, I meant…

SARAH

I'm a writer. A researcher, really. A consultant for other writers. I have a little office just down the street. I like to keep busy. I have a few clients here now.

STAN

She comes to every show. My audience enjoys seeing her almost as much as they come to see me. I dedicated the encore last season to her. "I've Grown Accustomed to Her Face."
                    (he starts to sing a few bars)

SARAH

(interrupting) Have either of you ever done any performing? Never been interested in it, myself. Happy behind the scenes. Stan needs me to be there.
                    (pauses, then looks at Robbie).
You know, you sort of look familiar to me. Are you a performer?

(LAURIE looks at ROBBIE, pours another glass, starts to swig it.
ROBBIE glares at her, takes a deep breath)

ROBBIE

Umm hmmm. Long time ago.

STAN

I'll never walk away from it. I'm getting better with each show. I keep refining my timing and pacing. It takes a lot of rehearsing to get a good performance under your belt. Some just have the gift, ya know?

SARAH

(*thinking*) Did you ever perform at the Blue Tango on West 46th?

ROBBIE

Uh, yeah.

SARAH

Wasn't it a tribute to....somebody..(*remembers it*) Ah, Rosemary Clooney!

ROBBIE

(*really doesn't want to talk about this*)

Yeah. Uh huh.

SARAH

We were there one night. We saw you. It was a couple of years ago, I think. Maybe more than that.

(*to Stan*)

Don't you remember her? Now I remember. You were good. We enjoyed it, didn't we, Stan?

STAN

(*disregarding the question*)

I've thought about doing a tribute show to Clooney. You don't have to be a woman to do it. I met Rosie once. Lovely person. She and I were in an elevator together one night and...

SARAH

(*interrupts; to ROBBIE*)

But you stopped?
> *(ROBBIE and LAURIE exchange looks)*

ROBBIE

Performing? Yeah. I teach intro courses in theater now at the university. More stable. Well... *(shrugs)*

STAN

I've directed lots of shows – all with famous cabaret people. That's teaching. I spent several summers at the Westgate Retreat Center working with cabaret students. I guess that makes me a master teacher. I'd like to find some students around here to work with.

LAURIE

At least, you don't have to worry about tenure.

SARAH
(to ROBBIE)

You aren't tenured?

> *(ROBBIE sips her wine, trying to decide how to respond to this unpleasant conversational gambit)*

ROBBIE
(clearly uncomfortable)

I don't want to...I don't think I can...This probably isn't the place to discuss...

SARAH
(realizing she might have stepped in it)

Oh. Sorry. *(pause)* Have you experienced any discrimination at the college because of...you know.

STAN

In New York, I never saw any at all outside the accounting group. Never in show business. Almost all my friends were gay or lesbian.

LAURIE

Robbie doesn't like that word.

SARAH

Lesbian? Why not?

ROBBIE

It's just a label. Doesn't describe who I am. And who we are. I'm not a subculture. People think it's all about flannel shirts and hating men.

LAURIE

It's just a word.

ROBBIE

No, it's not. Not really. It limits....

STAN
(interrupts)

Never mattered to me.

LAURIE

But you're straight....?

SARAH
(a little too quickly)

He most certainly is.

ROBBIE

While my friends were marching in gay rights parades, I worked behind the scenes. For a while, I volunteered for a state senator who....

STAN

(interrupts, a little too smugly)
People sometimes think I'm gay because I dress so fashionably.

SARAH

And because all your friends are gay. And you go to gay bars with them.

ROBBIE

Most of our friends are hetero. Just coincidental, really.

SARAH

Sorry, Robbie. I know the tenure is none of my business. *(almost to herself)* We've had a hard time making friends Here in L.A., haven't we, Stan? Don't understand it. We had good friends in New York.

ROBBIE

Is there any prejudice? Nah, I haven't seen it. At least, so far. It's not high on my list of things to worry about. *(beat, to SARAH)* Trouble making friends?

SARAH

Tenure's always a problem, isn't it? That's what I've heard. It's always good to get that awful process over with, I would think.

STAN

(getting bored as the conversation has moved away from him)
When I was at the accounting firm, all the junior partners came

to my shows. The senior partner even picked up the tab when they came to the last opening in New York.

SARAH

Then you were laid off a month later. You were so sure they enjoyed themselves that night.

STAN

There wasn't any connection, Sarah. The company was already over their heads in money problems. Of course, they loved the show. That was my Rodgers and Hammerstein. So many great ballads.
(*off in his own world*)
I especially loved....

ROBBIE
(*interrupting, challenging*)
Why did you two move here?

STAN

More chances to perform. New York is just a zoo. I know some of the bookers here in town. They all go to the Cabaret Conventions.
(*to LAURIE*)
I was glad the accountants didn't think I was one of them because I wasn't. They were all humorless and stiff. It gave me a chance to jump into what I really wanted to do, what I was born to do, to be honest.

SARAH

It's very expensive to live in Manhattan.

LAURIE

Yeah, I know.

SARAH

I had some scary health problems. Made it hard to get around to see doctors. Had to call 911 one night at rush hour and it took them almost an hour to get there in all that traffic. I was just lying there on the living room floor, waiting for someone to come.

LAURIE
(to STAN)

You must have been frantic.

SARAH

Oh, he wasn't there. Out with the boys.

STAN
(impatient)

Sarah, you know I was having dinner and drinks with the critic from the Village Voice. It was an important meeting. I worked to get that meeting for months.
(to LAURIE)
I was there when they loaded her into the ambulance. Very upsetting. It was horrible to see her like that.
(pause, sighs)
I miss the sophistication of New York.

(ROBBIE takes a deep breath, stifling a comment and glances at her watch as they sit in silence)

SARAH

Stan, we need to go. These people have to go to work tomorrow.

STAN

OK.

(everybody moves to the door)

LAURIE

It was good to meet you. I'm sure we'll be seeing each other again soon. Living so close. Glad we could finally get together after – what has it been? Two months?

STAN

I've been busy rehearsing, finding musicians. You know how it is.

(SARAH and LAURIE exchange knowing looks)

SARAH

Good luck with that tenure, Robbie.

STAN

I'll leave two tickets at the box office for you. Does Thursday, the 10th work for you? That's the second week.

LAURIE

I'll have to check. We'll get back to you tomorrow if that's OK.

STAN
(to ROBBIE)

You know, I bet we know some of the same people. Do you know Arthur Ekman? He books the Myriad Club on West 52nd. I had dinner with him last week. He's here for a month on vacation. He's coming to my show and bringing some friends. I'm sure it'll be a full house.

ROBBIE

No. Sorry, I don't.

STAN

Next time we get together we'll have to figure out who we both know.

ROBBIE

(smiles wanly)

Yeah. Maybe.

SARAH

It's not easy to meet people here. It's so spread out. Well, good night.

LAURIE, ROBBIE

Good night.

(SARAH and STAN exit, LAURIE begins to stack dishes and clean up; ROBBIE stands by the closed door, dazed)

LAURIE

Oh…my…God.

ROBBIE

Yeah. A real piece of work. I sure didn't want him to know I had been a performer. He doesn't have to know that. Don't want to go there. And I sure don't want to hear any more about his dumb little gigs, either. What an egomaniac. Can you imagine what he's like on stage? He didn't ask either of us a single question.

LAURIE

You seemed a little out of it tonight.

ROBBIE

I've been out of it?
(points to the now empty bottles on the table)
Sorry. Yeah, well. Jerry called me into his office today. I knew it was coming. The tenure talk.

LAURIE

It was obvious you didn't want to talk about it.

ROBBIE

I thought I had more time, maybe another year. I think I have all the academic bases covered, good student ratings and all that. Here's the problem. I have to produce some creative – something - that shows I know what I'm doing.

LAURIE

OK.

ROBBIE

Well, I don't. At least not as a playwright. It isn't enough that I'm a good teacher. Jerry says they want to see me write a play since theater is...what I do. It would be compelling evidence, he said. Tenure is competitive. There are others up, too.

LAURIE

OK.

ROBBIE

Never did it before. Playwriting wasn't part of my degree program. I had enough trouble writing my dissertation, much less a play. Remember all those extensions I got?

LAURIE

So what are you gonna do?

ROBBIE

I have no choice. Have to come up with something somehow - and soon.

LAURIE

What if you don't – can't?

ROBBIE

They'll keep me on until the end of the year. Then you'll have to support us again for a while until I can figure out what else I can do.

LAURIE

Oh God. Well, I've done it before; I can do it again. But...

ROBBIE

I know. I've appreciated that. Just have to come up with one good idea. Just one.

LAURIE

Sure hope it doesn't come to that. I didn't mind helping out when we were in New York because it seemed... time limited.

ROBBIE
(shocked)

Time limited?

LAURIE

You know what I mean. You were great, of course, but you know the odds. Everybody these days thinks they can sing.

And they all seemed so young. You hung in there longer than I thought you would.

ROBBIE

I thought you agreed it was worth doing.

LAURIE

I did. But it was a sort of a lark for you while I did the heavy lifting, to be truthful about it.

ROBBIE

A lark? Oh, I don't think I want to hear that. I thought you loved your job at the vet clinic. And I thought you wanted it for me as much as I did. You didn't say anything.

LAURIE

I did but you didn't want to talk about it. You might remember that I put in lots and lots of overtime at the office so we could live comfortably. I got tired. And I was missing you.

ROBBIE

Now I'm hearing about this.

LAURIE

I would have been more enthusiastic if things hadn't been so rough on you.

ROBBIE

Not easy to start a career as a performer at my age. Maybe I waited too long. I really wanted it.

LAURIE

I know.

ROBBIE

All this time, I thought you…

LAURIE

Rob, we'd been together long enough to know that you were the person I wanted to be with. I moved to New York to be with you. I left my business behind. My friends. I loved you. Love you. I wanted you to succeed. I still do. But there was nothing I could do to help. It wasn't my world at all. You were so wrapped up in those *people* and that lifestyle. 24/7. Then there was Betsy.

ROBBIE

What does that mean?

LAURIE

If we had stayed in New York, I think… I think we would have been history. Or, God forbid, we could've ended up like Stan and Sarah.

ROBBIE

Wait, wait. What about Betsy?

LAURIE

You two were way too close.

ROBBIE

She was my music director. Of course, we were close. We've had this conversation before.

LAURIE

So why am I not convinced? It still hurts, Rob. I worried about what you'd do to get ahead in that business.

ROBBIE

Could it be that your perception of all this was pickled in alcohol?

LAURIE

No. Not at all. An easy copout for you to say that. Not fair. And I don't drink that much. You're exaggerating.

ROBBIE

Laurie, I would never, ever cheat on you. I may have my faults but that isn't one of them. I love you and would never deliberately hurt...

LAURIE
(interrupts)
I have to admit there was a part of me that was relieved that last gig didn't go so well. I hate to say that, but you...
(stops, editing herself. She has said enough)

ROBBIE
(sinks into the couch, reliving the moment)
There were three people in the audience that last night.

LAURIE

I'm sorry you had to go through that. But it saved us. When you gave it up and took the job here, I could breathe for the first time since we left.

ROBBIE
(still in her reverie)
It was the one thing that mattered almost more than anything.

LAURIE

It was hard for me, too. You forget that.

ROBBIE

There was so much I didn't tell you. So much. There just wasn't time. The highs were unbelievable ... but the lows.... You didn't get the lows part, not the really bad ones. I didn't know if I would survive it. Sometimes, I wondered if I...

LAURIE

We almost didn't. There wasn't time for us.

ROBBIE

And that's when you started drinking too much. At least, that's when I noticed. I knew the history, but I thought it was under control. After that treatment program, it stopped. Done. And I wouldn't be bringing it up now if it was over with.

LAURIE
(defending herself)

I'd come home and you weren't there, night after night after night. You were gone almost every weekend. You were off with your friends or Betsy. What did you expect me to do?

ROBBIE

Oh, I dunno. Read? Watch TV? Come to my show?

LAURIE

Are you blaming me for New York? That's all over. We're on a better path now. Real life.

ROBBIE
(back in the reverie)

I wonder if anything is ever really over.

LAURIE

It's those people who brought it up tonight. Stan is a part of that crazy world. Sarah was being pushy.

ROBBIE

Yeah. It's too unfinished. Don't want to deal with any of it.

LAURIE

I feel better about us now. Good. Solid. We have savings, investments, a future.

ROBBIE

Somewhere in there I feel like I lost a big chunk of myself.

LAURIE

Now you have a job that pays a salary. Your students love you.

ROBBIE

Well.
(doesn't want to continue this)
I really need this tenure thing to happen so I, so we, don't have to do any of that again.

LAURIE
(goes over and hugs ROBBIE)
I'll clean up the mess.

ROBBIE

Let's do it tomorrow
(points to the stuff left on the table).
It's late. I need more time to think, come up with an idea. I'll be there in a while.

*(LAURIE takes some stuff into the kitchen while ROBBIE
returns to the couch and sits)*

Lights down

SCENE TWO

*ROBBIE and LAURIE's living room. It's several weeks later, late
Saturday morning. Laundry is piled up on the sofa ready to take
to the laundry room. ROBBIE is sitting on the sofa, finishing her
coffee while reading the paper. LAURIE enters with her own cup
and a carafe for refills.*

ROBBIE
(laughing, quoting)

"Mr. Schneiderman, new to the LA cabaret scene, gives his
audience a challenging evening unfortunately dominated by
his uncertain intonation." Oh, my God. Can't sing, can't act,
clumsy, panders to the audience. When he tried to dance – well.
I worried he might fall off the stage. Musicians were wonderful,
though. Guess I thought the players here wouldn't be as good
as they are in New York.

LAURIE

I lost count of the number of times he forgot the words. The
piano player had to keep cuing him. I didn't dare look at you.
It would have been a disaster *(laughing)*.

ROBBIE

The only mystery for me is how did he do it in New York? He makes it sound like he was the Noel Coward of the cabaret community. Of course, Noel's been dead a long time. Makes comparisons easier.

LAURIE

Now we have to figure out something positive to say to him. How about, "Now THAT was a show!" Or "I've never seen anything quite like it." I've never been good at telling someone who's lousy that they're good. And I've had lots of practice.

(they exchange looks)

ROBBIE

I found it odd that he seemed to sing so many songs with double entendre lyrics. Isn't he too old for that? Ech.

LAURIE

I wondered how the audience felt. You know who I really felt sorry for? Sarah. She sat in the back and watched him the whole time. I guess she's there every night. That would be tough.

ROBBIE
(folding up the paper)
Hey, didn't get a chance to tell you that I met again with Jerry yesterday afternoon.

LAURIE

And? Anything new?

ROBBIE

Oh, yeah. The tenure committee meets way before the end of the school year. I have less time than I thought. I need to do this – like yesterday. I've been thinking about it, reading stuff. Trying to get ideas…

LAURIE

Hey, I have an idea. Why don't you write about me?

(an awkward pause)

ROBBIE

(laughs)

You? How is that a good idea?

LAURIE

(framing it with her hands like a director)

The high school dropout who goes through Betty Ford as a teenager, comes back to make it through college and veterinary school. Don't you think that would be inspiring? Then we met. And…

ROBBIE

…The malpractice suit hanging over our heads because you were drunk during surgery with that German shepherd, returning to drinking every night again.

LAURIE

Hey, cut me some slack here. I've had a lot of stress at work. And I wasn't drunk, either. They can't prove that.

ROBBIE

You aren't worried about the lawsuit?

LAURIE

Not really. It's all hearsay.

ROBBIE

Sometimes when you come home from work, you seem so...I don't know...preoccupied.

LAURIE

I know. We've had too many deaths these past few months. I know these things go in cycles, but it's still hard. I get attached to the little guys.

ROBBIE

Then you put up photos of them on the refrigerator door. Doesn't that make you feel worse? Why do you do that to yourself?

LAURIE

You keep all those posters from your singing career. What's the difference?

ROBBIE

(*waves her off*)
Actually, I have an idea for a character I can build the play around. And, no, it's not you. You're a character, all right, but not for this.

LAURIE

Yeah? Who? A real person?

ROBBIE

Sort of.
(*ROBBIE smiles at LAURIE, a beat, then LAURIE gets it*)

LAURIE

Stan??? Oh, no. Really?

ROBBIE

He's perfect. He's like a cartoon character. He is so full of him-self – and for no good reason. It could be a very funny play.

LAURIE

Oh, no.

ROBBIE

Why are you so negative? I think it's a great idea. I'm just relieved I came up with it.

LAURIE

You're going to make up stuff about him?

ROBBIE
(chuckles)
I don't think I'll have to. He has told us enough about himself to give me a pretty good start on it. And that embarrassing show...! I wonder how I can work that in....

LAURIE

You're going to write a play about our next-door neighbor?

ROBBIE

This is a perfect solution to my problem, our problem. And the best part is it will write itself.

LAURIE

I don't know....

ROBBIE

The worst part is that I'll have to spend more time with him. It'd be better if I could use his own words. Some of the things he says....He's never asked me anything about my show biz career. Clearly, he has no interest beyond The World of Stan. It's a great start to a very funny show. Hey, there's my title: The World of Stan. Or, A Life Without Talent. It's gonna be great.

LAURIE

It seems so, I don't know, disrespectful. You've never done anything like this before – have you? I don't like it.

ROBBIE

Come on, Laurie. I have to do this. It's not that I haven't sweated over this, trying to come up with something. And here it is – right next door. It's like a gift, all wrapped up under a bright, shiny Christmas tree with a star on top.

(turns and walks to the autographed baseball on the desk and brings it over to LAURIE)

Do you really think Joe DiMaggio signed this ball? I'll bet he had some little old lady do it. Maybe he paid her 25 cents a signature. She sat in her worn-out Lazy Boy chair in her drafty living room wrapped in her shawl, carefully signing each ball. And you can be sure he got his cut before she got paid. She made a little money and he became even more famous, the darling of the fans. They loved him because they thought he cared about them. Sometimes being close to reality is close enough. So who loses in something like that?
(places ball on coffee table)
Nobody.

LAURIE

I don't know. We've shared meals, drinks. Seems like it's using a friend...

ROBBIE
(*surprised*)
You think of him – them – as friends?

LAURIE
Yeah, I do. Well, maybe more Sarah than Stan.

ROBBIE
(*shakes her head, deep breath*)
OK. Let me put it this way. If I can write a comedy about somebody we know…and it could even turn out to be good and secure our future forever….I wouldn't have to write another play – ever.

LAURIE
(*sigh*)
It just doesn't seem…Can't think of the right word. We're going to have dinners with them, pretend to be friends and all the while you'll be pumping him and collecting anecdotes for your play. Right?

ROBBIE
You got it. That's it.

LAURIE
I don't know if I can do it. Are you going to take notes at dinner?

ROBBIE
Please.

LAURIE
I wish there was another way.

ROBBIE

There's no time to screw around with this. Besides, even if he knew – and -

(she emphasizes this)

he must never, ever know – don't you think he'd be more puffed up than ever? The thought that someone thinks he's fascinating enough to write about? For him, it'd be like starring in a show. Getting a Tony. I think it's inspired. Not sure of the plot points yet, but what a wonderful character to build the play around. I'm working on that. He's surprisingly...interesting. Listen, Laurie, once I get tenure, we can get that dog, that small one. You've been wanting one forever, right?

LAURIE

Yeah.

(shakes her head in resignation)

ROBBIE

The play's just an academic exercise. He'll never see it because it'll never be produced. All I have to do is to submit it to the committee. That's it. It's the last piece of the tenure jigsaw puzzle. Then, I'm as good as tenured.

(Knock at the door. LAURIE answers the door. It's STAN)

STAN

Hi. Sorry to barge in. You busy?

LAURIE

(obviously uncomfortable at the timing)

No, no. Come in. We were just talking about you. About your show. Sit down.

ROBBIE
(delighted to see him)
We're having coffee. Want some?

STAN
Sure. I'll take a cup. Kinda convenient to be right next door.

(LAURIE goes out to get it)

ROBBIE
Sarah sleeping in?

STAN
Yeah. An old habit from coming to my late-night Friday shows. Had a good house last night. I'm still revved up from the show, I guess. Bounced up early.

(LAURIE returns with his coffee and a bottle of brandy)

LAURIE
I thought maybe you'd like some of this liquid alarm clock.

ROBBIE
(not happy)
Isn't a little early?

LAURIE
Just a little friendly brandy.

STAN
Too early in the day for me. But you go ahead. I only drink at night after the show. Any alcohol interferes with my ability to perform.

177

(The silence is uncomfortable. Both LAURIE and ROBBIE know why he is here. LAURIE pours some of the brandy into her coffee, offers the bottle to ROBBIE who demurs)

LAURIE

We appreciated leaving us the comps. Looked like you had an OK crowd. I guess it'll get better, right?

STAN

The house manager papered the room. It's just a matter of time before audiences here will have heard of Stan Schneiderman. It's only been a couple of months. The word will get around.

LAURIE

(trying to think of something positive to say)
You could tell you enjoy doing that.

STAN

(eats it up)
I love it. It's the best place in the world to be – on stage. My natural milieu.

ROBBIE

The photo of you near the door made you look very handsome. Oh, not that you aren't. Taken a while back, no?

STAN

I need to have new publicity photos taken here. Several poses, different looks.
(moving on to why he's really there)
So. Did you have a favorite song in the show? Something you particularly loved?

ROBBIE
(looks at LAURIE)
I always enjoy hearing "Anything Goes."

STAN
Yeah. I get tired of hearing the sanitized version that everybody knows. Cole knew a little dirt never hurt anybody. Did you two notice the trouble I had moving around on stage?

LAURIE
(confused)
No, not at all. Why?

STAN
It's these damned hemorrhoids. They're back. Sitting, standing. Doing just about anything. I can forget about them when I'm singing or telling a story, but when I move – hurts like hell. Whole body hurts. I probably need to see a doctor. I've been putting it off. Back hurts, too.

(weak smiles, not knowing what to say)

LAURIE
I'm sure nobody noticed you. Well, you know what I mean.

ROBBIE
Yeah, after that review in the Outlook, wow. The turnout was pretty good, considering. Papering the place was good insurance.

LAURIE
That was terrible, what the reviewer said. She doesn't know how hard it is to remember lyrics under the pressure of performing.

STAN

She was just there on an off night. It happens. I don't read that stuff.

ROBBIE

She was pretty devastating, talking about all the intonation problems you were having. What was the quote? "His notes were like pinatas being attacked by a blindfolded singer"? Awful.

(STAN wants to change the subject, notices the baseball, picks it up)

STAN

Who's the baseball fan?

LAURIE

We both are. Yankees in New York, Dodgers here. But the ball's Robbie's.

STAN
(examining it)

He signed it, huh?

ROBBIE

I'd like to think so, considering what I paid for it. There's a certificate of authenticity around here somewhere but....

STAN

It's probably like those old movie star 8X10 glossies the studios sent out in the good old days. Some studio lackey signed them. I wish I had an autographed ball from, oh, Betty Grable or Barbara Stanwyck. Or Noel Coward.
(he laughs; Laurie and Robbie exchange looks).

I had some autographs from stars when I was a kid in Philadelphia. My mother threw them away when I went to camp.

ROBBIE

What was important back then was they had what they thought was the real thing.

(LAURIE, increasingly uncomfortable, pours more brandy into her cup, without needing the coffee)

STAN

We thought they were all wonderful. Beautiful, rich, glamorous, happy. And most of them weren't happy at all. They were a mess.

ROBBIE

Even the bios were made up. And their names.

STAN

Well, they couldn't let Joan Crawford go on as Lucille LeSueur, after all, which sounded too much like sewer.

ROBBIE

Loved her. From what I read, her real life was like her roles – driven, uncompromising.

STAN

Always the career. It was all that mattered to her. She paid a price. Her life didn't end well.

ROBBIE

The public never knew.

STAN

It was all about the illusion. Bigger than life.

ROBBIE

The lies and deception served a bigger purpose, didn't they?
And no one died.

(laughs)

LAURIE

What about the movie stars who couldn't live with the lies
anymore and killed themselves?

ROBBIE

(looking at Laurie)

Then there were those who drank and drugged themselves to
death.

STAN

Tragedy behind the scenes but what fabulous movies they made.
Worth it, I'd say.

ROBBIE

I completely agree.

STAN

Hey, maybe you could come back and see the show again this week.

LAURIE

Uh. I'm not sure we....

ROBBIE

I wouldn't worry about audience turnout. Nobody reads that
local paper, anyway.

STAN

(gets up)

Yeah. Gotta run. Just wanted to thank you guys for coming. Glad you loved the show.

ROBBIE

Oh, we sure did. Didn't we, Laurie?

LAURIE

(reluctant and aware she's starting to feed into the plot) Yeah, we did.

STAN

I'm over there working on memorizing new songs for the next few days, so if you don't see me... I have papers and music arrangements spread all over the floor, putting together the new show. I love doing that. It's going to be spectacular. New spin on old songs. Younger audiences need to hear them. Society needs to hear them.

(ROBBIE and LAURIE walk him to the door)

ROBBIE

Good luck with the new show. Can hardly wait.

(he leaves)

LAURIE

That was awkward.

ROBBIE

Have to figure out a way to get him to talk about himself in more pompous terms. I need dialogue. I want him to think we're fans so he'll trust me. I think he's starting to. That talk about hemorrhoids and backaches.

LAURIE

Trust you? That's an interesting concept.

ROBBIE

Come to think of it, how can I trust you?

LAURIE

What? What do you mean?

ROBBIE

Once you start drinking, your mouth seems to have a motor in it. How do I know you won't blurt something out?

LAURIE

I wouldn't do that.

ROBBIE

You say that now. You've embarrassed me before. I don't know. That would screw everything up.
(pause for effect)
And I mean everything. This is important for both of us. It's for us.

LAURIE

I know. I know you say that, but...

ROBBIE

I'm going to go start the laundry. Why don't you just sit here and finish off your little friend?
(nods at the brandy bottle)

(She's disgusted, of course, LAURIE a little ashamed. ROBBIE exits. LAURIE watches her go, then pours a drink. As she does, she "accidentally" spills some on the baseball)

Lights Down.

SCENE THREE

(LAURIE and ROBBIE's condo, three months later. It's close to Christmas. There's a small, decorated tree in the corner, with wrapped gifts under it. ROBBIE is at the desk with papers all over, typing, as LAURIE comes in the front door)

LAURIE

Hi.

ROBBIE

Hey. I'm almost done with the first act here.

LAURIE

How's it coming?

ROBBIE

Great! We had lunch together today and he went on and on about all his famous "friends." I'm sure these people barely know he exists, but he sure does think he's special. God's gift to the entertainment world. All grist for the mill. I really don't need much more of Stan's input. This whole process is turning out to be really fun, at least the writing part. I don't know why I haven't written a play before. You want to read it?

LAURIE

Maybe when you're done.

(*LAURIE heads to the kitchen*)

Want a glass of wine before dinner?

ROBBIE

No, thanks. I want to finish this up tonight. I have way more quotes than I need to flesh out the character. But I need a really good final scene.

(*LAURIE exits, returns with a glass and a bottle of wine*)

ROBBIE
(*looking at the pages*)
Brings back old memories. Writing about being on stage. I try to keep it at arm's length by making it funny, but –

LAURIE

Do you miss it? The performing?

ROBBIE

No. Yeah. I don't know any more.

(*knock at door. It's STAN and SARAH*)

SARAH

Hi. Are we interrupting? We were running errands. I thought we were just getting appetizers, but Stan picked up more than we can eat. It's just dim sum.

STAN

The place reminds me of New York. Quick, cheap and not terrible. Yes?

LAURIE

Sure. Thanks. Sit.

STAN

We can't stay long. Have to get back to working on the new show. It's coming along really well. Another winner.

(They all sit down with the food on their laps. Wine is poured.)

ROBBIE

So, Stan. I've been meaning to ask you. How did you get started in cabaret?

(LAURIE and ROBBIE exchange looks)

STAN

It was fate. Absolutely meant to be. My parents always asked me to entertain their friends at their parties. I had an uncle who taught me songs he knew the adults would enjoy. You know, I still sing some of them. I've always been an entertainer, in demand. Kismet.

ROBBIE

You always knew you'd be a star, huh?

LAURIE

I'm sure Stan doesn't want to relive his history over dim sum.

STAN

Oh, I'm fine with that. Maybe I could be an inspiration to your students.

ROBBIE

Oh, yes. An inspiration.

SARAH

Speaking of performing, Stan has some big news.

ROBBIE

What's that?

STAN

I bought a club!

ROBBIE

(shocked) Really?

STAN

It was a natural, an easy decision. A place to showcase my talent. It'll take some work to get the audiences back there. It's not in bad shape but no one has appeared on that stage for several years. I got it cheap.

SARAH

I had a small inheritance from my father. With our savings, he could pay cash for it.

STAN

I can get it cleaned out, make some minor cosmetic changes and have it ready for a show in six weeks or so.

LAURIE

Wow. That's very exciting.

ROBBIE

I don't know what to say. That's a major change. Big risk, sounds like.

STAN

Now I'll always have a place to do my shows. Sarah will handle the publicity, the office work, all the details while I entertain every weekend. Did the deal a couple of days ago.

(ROBBIE is frozen at this unexpected turn of events, while LAURIE seems excited by the news)

SARAH

We're counting on Stan being able to bring in enough money to take care of expenses, both at the club and here. Once he's up and running, that is.

ROBBIE

Wow. I don't know what to say.

STAN

My new show will be written by next week and I'll have plenty of time to polish it up before the grand opening. I wonder if we can bring in a few Klieg lights.

SARAH

Oh, Stan. You promised no more expenses.
(looks over at the desk)

So many papers. Been busy working? You're certainly neater than Stan.

(She moves her chair closer to the desk. ROBBIE hurries over and cuts her off)

ROBBIE

Oh, just some notes for a lecture. Have to keep ahead of the students, you know.

STAN
(Gets up, moves toward the desk)
I'd be happy to help. You know I gave a lecture once to a class.

ROBBIE
(leaps up to sit on the desk to block his access)
Oh, no, no, no. That's fine. Everything's under control.

SARAH

How's that tenure coming along?

ROBBIE

Oh, fine. Good. Good.

LAURIE

She's working on it.

STAN

I hope you'll both come to the club often. It'd be good to have friends in the audience. I'll give you a discount.

ROBBIE
(can think of little worse than this).

Sure. Sure. Thanks.

STAN

Laurie, maybe you can post some fliers at your office. Dog lovers would love me. Cat people, too. And Robbie, I know your students would get my shows. I could come to your classes and do something, like a song and some patter so they'd know what to expect. I need to think about planting publicity all over the city. I wonder if I have time for a little nip and tuck.

SARAH
(disgusted)
And where will we get the money for that? There's not much left.

STAN

This could make me big. *(think Norma Desmond)* Bigger.

ROBBIE

If you'll excuse me, I really need to get back to work. That, uh, lecture happens at the end of the week.

(she tries to herd them toward the door, away from the desk)

LAURIE

Thanks for the unexpected snacks.

SARAH

Glad you hadn't had dinner. Always good to get together. Sorry we have to nosh and run.

(LAURIE sees them to the door)

LAURIE

Congrats on the exciting news.

(all say their good-byes and STAN and SARAH exit.
ROBBIE goes to the desk and sits)

ROBBIE

Wow, that was close. Nobody saw anything. He bought a club? Oh, my God. What is he thinking?

LAURIE

He's just trying to be a success. Like you are.

ROBBIE

(she walks to the desk, writes)
Wait. I need to make a few notes. A club? Really? Doesn't that seem, oh, I don't know,.grandiose? And he'll be the only performer? *(Laughs)* I can imagine how long that will last. And it's their life savings, too? Sarah didn't sound all that happy about it, either. Oh, my God. I suppose it hadn't occurred to him that I could....

(loud pounding on the door. They startle and run to the door.
STAN is standing there with the bottom of his pants soaking
wet)

STAN

We're flooded.

LAURIE, ROBBIE

What? Huh?

STAN

I think a pipe broke in the guest bath. Can Sarah stay here while I go back and check the damage?

LAURIE

Oh, no. I'm so sorry. I'll get some towels.
(she leaves to do that, returns quickly with several)

*(STAN leaves, returns in a moment pushing SARAH.
They are both upset)*

LAURIE
(to SARAH)

Are you OK?

ROBBIE

Let me put some towels on the rug for you
(near her chair).

SARAH

It's just a little water, that's all. Good thing we put the cat down before we came to LA. She'd have hated this.

LAURIE

What a shock.

STAN
(starts to leave)

I'll be back in a few minutes. What do I do? In New York, I'd call the super.

ROBBIE

The property manager might be home downstairs.

STAN

I need to walk through the condo first. To see how bad it is.

(out the door)

LAURIE

(calls to him)

Be careful. It's probably slippery in there.

SARAH

We're insured. At least, I think we are. It's not our fault a pipe broke. Is it? Do you think it flooded the condo below us?

LAURIE

You'll know soon enough. What will you do? You have family here?

SARAH

Our families are in New York, what's left of them.

LAURIE

Let me get more wine.

(LAURIE leaves to get more wine, returns with another bottle, uncorks it)

ROBBIE

(sarcastically)

Oh, that'll help everything.

SARAH

I could use a glass, if there's enough.

ROBBIE

We seem to have an infinite supply.

(STAN walks in without knocking, carrying a big pile of water-logged papers)

STAN

Sorry.

LAURIE

That's OK.

SARAH

How bad is it?

STAN

My music arrangements and most of my notes have dissolved in the water. I don't have copies, either. I was going to get them copied tomorrow.
(moans)
Why did this have to happen to me?

SARAH

I meant the condo, Stan.

STAN

Oh. There's only an inch or two of water but it's everywhere. I think the master bath is still dry, ironically. The clothes in the closet are OK but the shoes probably won't make it.

SARAH

We have insurance, right?

STAN

(exasperated)

Yeah, but it doesn't cover my artistic work.

ROBBIE

You might want to talk to the manager to see what they do in a situation like this. I mean, after cleaning it up.

STAN

I could call some friends in New York. They might have some music charts I can use.

SARAH

They have their own lives, Stan. They wouldn't send you arrangements they paid good money for. And they wouldn't be in your key, anyway. I can't believe I said that. We have to think about the house, not your damned music.

STAN

I'm paying a very high price for being creative.

LAURIE

I hope they can get the water out quickly so you can get back in.

STAN

Me, too.

LAURIE

Do you have friends in LA?

SARAH

Just you two. There are the Jamisons down the hall but they are cranky and...

STAN

... they have no appreciation for the arts at all. They didn't even come to my show. Terrible people.

LAURIE

Maybe there's an empty unit in the building.

ROBBIE

No. It's full up, as of last June. There's a Residence Inn not too far from here.

SARAH

I don't know how we'd be able to afford that. What are we going to do, Stan?

STAN

Remember Frank DeLuca, the Brooklyn Baritone? He came to a couple of my shows in New York. I remember him telling me he had a flood at his house, and it took the insurance company only a few months to cough up the reimbursement. I think he got money for a hotel within a week. He came to my Gershwin show right after that. Loved it. You know, where I sang...

SARAH

How long can we stay at the Residence Inn?

STAN

(preoccupied with his wet papers)

I don't know.

ROBBIE

(looking at LAURIE)

Listen. We have an extra bedroom. If you need to stay here for a couple of nights that would be OK with us. Right, Laurie?

LAURIE
(not happy)
What? Oh, sure, sure. A couple of nights.

ROBBIE
It's the Christmas season, after all. You don't want to be in a hotel.

SARAH
You really don't have to...

STAN
Oh, good. I'm going to go back to see what I can bring over here to dry.

SARAH
I'll go downstairs and find the manager while you do that.

LAURIE
I can come along, if you'd like.

STAN
No need. She's very independent.

SARAH
I've had to be. Thanks, Laurie. I'm OK.

ROBBIE
We'll give you our spare key.
(STAN and SARAH leave)

(A beat. LAURIE staring daggers at ROBBIE)

ROBBIE

I had to say something. They have no place to go.

LAURIE

Neither do I. Our condo isn't that big. Isn't our life complicated enough as it is? We'll have zero privacy.

ROBBIE

Yeah, I know. But this is just what I needed. He'll be more un-guarded here. Oh, I know. I hadn't planned on living together, either. It was just like this opportunity dropped in my lap. Our laps. Golden. Maybe I can find a good ending for the play.

LAURIE

Well, if it's just a couple of days...Still feels a little like an invasion.

(STAN bursts in without knocking with another huge pile of water-logged papers in a large cardboard box)

STAN

Since I'm staying here now, I guess I can come in without knocking.
  (puts the box down on the carpet, begins to take out the wet papers, starts to spread them all over the living room).
Can I lay these out here somewhere?

(LAURIE and ROBBIE look at each other)

Act One Curtain

Act Two

SCENE ONE

ROBBIE and LAURIE's condo, five weeks later. It's cluttered, having the look of too many people in too small a space. There are papers, books piled everywhere. On top of the desk is a portable music keyboard, crowding the computer into a corner of the desk. There's a music stand by the desk, filled with music, hindering access. Some of STAN's clothes are draped across the end of the sofa. It's dark when LAURIE enters from outside. She flips on the lights and wakes up ROBBIE who has been asleep on the sofa.

ROBBIE
(groggy but impatient; rises)
Where the hell have you been? What's....

LAURIE
(clearly intoxicated)
It's over. Suspended for two years. No surgery, no treatment. The good news? No more lawsuit. The bad news? Have to be supervised by another licensed vet. I'm back to being a lowly tech. And back to rehab. Part of the deal. Lousy, if you ask me.

*(ROBBIE gets up, LAURIE looks around for a drink, finds
the bottle and pours herself a tall one; refreshes throughout this
scene)*

ROBBIE

When we talked at the break, you said things were going well.

LAURIE

There was that other problem with the Boston terrier in New York. And some others. They found out, blindsided me. If it had just been the collie…

ROBBIE

(moves to hug her, now can smell the alcohol)
The hearing ended hours ago. I've been here, waiting. No call, no nothing. You shut off your cell?

LAURIE

Didn't feel like talking.

ROBBIE

Looks like you felt like drinking. Aren't things bad enough? You didn't drive home, I hope.

LAURIE

(shakes her head "no")
I ran into Shelly and John outside the Administration building. They didn't know and I didn't tell them.

ROBBIE

Yeah, you don't need another DUI. I honestly don't know what to say.

LAURIE

So what now, she asks. What now? What now?

ROBBIE

Yeah.

LAURIE

Totally up to you now, Rob. Gonna leave me?

ROBBIE

(*pauses, a measured response*)
No. Why do you take this to the limit all the time? It's awful timing, that's all. My play goes to the tenure committee tomorrow morning. I need to get some sleep. You, too.

LAURIE

You finished it?

ROBBIE

Yeah. The only good thing about Stan being here is that it speeded up the process.
(*hugs her*)
Hey, we'll get through this. We always have.

LAURIE

Yeah. You go to bed. I'm going to sit up for a while.

(*ROBBIE studies her, decides not to pursue anything and exits; LAURIE dims the lights, returns to the sofa, pours another drink. SARAH enters from the hall. LAURIE turns to see her*)

SARAH

Sorry. Didn't mean to startle you. Stan's snoring like a lumber-jack in there.

LAURIE

It's OK. Train wrecks are fascinating. Wanna drink?

SARAH

Sure. Can't sleep anyway.
                    (LAURIE finds a glass and pours her one;
                        they both continue to drink).
I'm sorry we've been here so long. Stan said the inspection will
be done by the end of the week. Sure hope so. I know this has
been a huge imposition.

LAURIE

(nods, shrugs, doesn't care) Doesn't matter.

SARAH

I'm sorry. You have enough going on without....

LAURIE

You're sorry a lot, aren't you, Sarah?

SARAH

(pauses) Yeah, I guess I am.

LAURIE

Me, too.

SARAH

Not always easy being married to a...a...

LAURIE
(snorts a little)
I can imagine.

SARAH

But you…

LAURIE

Yeah, I've got one of those, too. Different cloak, different name….same fixation.

SARAH

Yeah, both performers.

LAURIE

Oh, no. Not Robbie. She doesn't perform any more.

SARAH

Maybe not now.

LAURIE

Nah, she's done. She likes what she's doing. She's a good teacher. She'll get tenure, too. Wait and see.

SARAH

Having lived with Stan all these years, I know it's never over. Like an infection. Doesn't ever go away. Circumstances can change.

LAURIE
(shakes her head "no")

SARAH

I wasn't always in this chair, you know.

LAURIE

Oh, man. I never asked. I wouldn't…

SARAH

Stan did this.

LAURIE

Stan? Oh, no. He did this? Can I ask what happened?

SARAH

I was going with him to a TV interview. Running late as usual. He was rehearsing a monologue, in his own little world. Ran a red light. He was fine, of course. Always lands on his feet. The other driver and I got the worst of it. He was lucky nobody died. Both cars totaled. The other guy didn't even sue him. Should have, too. He never even...apologized to me. He said it was the other guy's fault. Of course.

LAURIE

Jeez, Sarah. You stayed with him after that? How could you do that?

SARAH

I needed his help for a long time. I was very angry. Still am. But he'll never leave me. He owes me.

LAURIE

Yeah.

SARAH

I probably shouldn't have said anything. Please don't tell Robbie. I don't want this to end up in her play.

LAURIE
(*startles*)

What?

SARAH

Oh, Laurie. I know. Have for a while.

LAURIE

You know? But how?

SARAH

I wasn't snooping. Honestly. It was easy to put it together when I saw the script on the desk. The tenure pressure, the invitation to stay here.

LAURIE

My turn to be sorry, I guess. You have to know I never wanted this.

SARAH

Don't be. He doesn't know. No need to tell him.

LAURIE

It isn't him I'm worried about. If Robbie finds out, she'll think I told you.

SARAH
(laughs)

She captures him perfectly. He is insensitive but he has a few endearing qualities here and there. I admit I was…upset, angry at first when I saw it. I thought maybe you invited us here just so she could…use…Stan to get what she needed at work.

LAURIE

Oh, no, that's not why…

SARAH

But everybody uses and gets used, don't they, Laurie? You and I, for instance. I know Robbie wasn't a big hit in New York, so you must have worked hard to help her get what she wanted.

LAURIE

I did. You're right.

SARAH

I've always helped Stan, too. Set aside my own life sometimes. That's what we do, isn't it? When we love someone. It evens out in the end. Sometimes.

LAURIE

I guess it does. So you're not mad about the play?

SARAH

Not really. Not anymore. What I read was very funny. Stan is a comical person but, you know, he's very loyal. To me and to other people. I appreciate that. I think you are, too. You're a good person, Laurie. Don't worry about it.

LAURIE
(almost panicked)
If Rob finds out, she'll think I told you about Stan. That would be worse than awful.

SARAH

It'll be our secret. I suspect we both have a lot of those. Now we share a bond of sorts, don't we?

LAURIE
(feeling the booze and the weight of the day)

I can't deal with this. I think I need to go to bed. This has been one of the worst days of my life.

SARAH

Ah, you're young. There will be more – maybe even some better days.

LAURIE
(goes to hug SARAH)
You're really OK with this play being about Stan?

SARAH

Let's just call it Karma. Good night.

(SARAH exits. LAURIE stands in the middle of the room, stunned by all the day's events. She turns off the lights.)

Lights Down

SCENE TWO

A few days later. Lights up on the messy condo. It's obvious the houseguests haven't completely left yet. ROBBIE, LAURIE and SARAH all sit in the living room. Diet and regular sodas fill the table, along with wine glasses and a bottle.

SARAH

I'm sorry this has taken so long. Bet you'll be glad when we're outta here tomorrow.

LAURIE

It's been hard on all of us.

SARAH

When does your rehab program start?

LAURIE

I'm on a waiting list. It's a 30-day program and it could take that long to get into it. Part of the deal with the Board. I'm starting now, though.

SARAH

Stopping any addiction is hard.

ROBBIE

Tell me about it. Hope it works this time. Is this number three or four?

(STAN enters without knocking; all greet him; he's glum)

SARAH

Hi. What did you find out? How close are you to being ready to open?

STAN

Couple more weeks. We finally have a firm opening date.
(he sits)

ROBBIE

Why so down? What's wrong?

SARAH

He went to the doctor today.

LAURIE

The doctor? What....

STAN

She's sidelined me for three months. Three months! No performing. It's just a little disk issue.

SARAH

Little? You've been having trouble moving around at all, driving, lots of things. I worry about all those pain pills.

LAURIE

What are you going to do?

STAN

I don't know yet. I have to open on time. The bills keep coming in, whether I'm working or not.

LAURIE

Can't you get someone from New York to fill in for a while? One of your friends?

STAN

I've called everybody. They're all busy.

SARAH

Or they say they are. It's asking a lot for them to come out here to work in a new club, Stan. You'd have to pay all their expenses, too.

STAN

Hey, maybe I could do the show from the couch. Sort of "Marlene Dietrich" sexy. The club *has* to open.

(everyone rolls their eyes at the thought of this)

SARAH

(an "aha" moment) Robbie!

ROBBIE

Yeah?

SARAH

Robbie. Do you still have your arrangements for the Clooney show?

(silence for a bit)

LAURIE

Here we go.

ROBBIE

(surprised, trying to take this all in; unsure)

I do.

STAN

Sarah, I'll be fine. No need to bring in a sub.

SARAH

You're not fine. We could lose our shirts. You know I wasn't happy about this from the start. You need to be practical. For once.

STAN

OK. OK. If I can't do it, you're the next best thing.

SARAH

High praise, indeed. If begrudging. But a great idea.

LAURIE
(to ROBBIE)
You're not seriously considering this.

*(She makes eye contact with SARAH who shrugs as if saying,
I told you so")*

ROBBIE
I. Don't. Know.
(to STAN, taking this in, smiles)
You really want me to open your club?

STAN
Just for a month or so until I can talk the doc into a medical
release. You wouldn't start for three weeks. That gives you time
to find musicians, rehearse, get your chops back.

*(LAURIE abruptly stalks out of the room into
the kitchen/bedroom area)*

SARAH
I know it's out of the blue. He wouldn't ask if it weren't....
urgent. I don't know what else we can do. We have a lot on
the line financially.

ROBBIE
(looks off for LAURIE)
I don't know. It's complicated. Stakes are high here, too.

SARAH
I understand. Stan, I think we should go out for a while and
leave them alone to discuss this.

STAN

Hmmm, yeah, OK. Oh, The marquee would read, "Stan Schneiderman Presents" and then your name. The type would be just a little smaller.

ROBBIE

I don't know. I don't know.

SARAH

Think about it, won't you? Let us know as soon as you can.

(SARAH follows STAN to the exterior door and they exit)

ROBBIE

Shit, shit, shit, shit.
(paces around the living room, sees the baseball and picks it up, tosses it up and down)

LAURIE

(enters, points to the ball)

See, there's the problem right there. That's what caused us to get caught up in their crazy world. You and your illusion versus reality. You're sabotaging us.

ROBBIE

If I did this – and I'm not saying I would – I could do it at night and still teach during the day. It wouldn't interfere with anything, really.

LAURIE

What about us?

ROBBIE

You won't even be here.

LAURIE

Meaning you can't come to the family meetings in the evenings.

ROBBIE

No loss there. How many times can we go over the same old pop psychy crap? This is about you, not me.

LAURIE

But it always seems to come around to being about you, doesn't it? You always get what you want.

ROBBIE

That's not true.

LAURIE

I've gone along. I've always gone along. You wanted the singing career in New York. You wanted to come back to LA. You wanted to use our friends as fodder for your play. Now you want more. Always more.

ROBBIE

I wanted it for us.

LAURIE

You say that. Rob. I need you to be there....

ROBBIE

I'm here. I'm not going anywhere.

LAURIE

I'm going to be a lousy vet tech for two years. Know how that feels?

ROBBIE

Don't blame me for that. You did that to yourself.

LAURIE

Somewhere in here, we've lost all our...

ROBBIE

Let's not pull the pin on the grenade. Stan made me an offer. That's all.

LAURIE

You're going to do it, aren't you?

ROBBIE

Let me ask you this. If you could magically get your license back - shazam - and have all the sanctions removed, would you do it, no matter what?

LAURIE

You want it.

ROBBIE

I think I have to give it another try. I don't want to live with regret forever. Stan owes me this.

LAURIE

He *what?*

ROBBIE

I've put up with him for over a month and it's payback time.

LAURIE

You know, this wasn't his idea. It came from Sarah.

ROBBIE

Doesn't matter to me.

LAURIE

For her it's all about the money. She doesn't know the trouble
she.....
(*then realizes she does*)
If we're talking balance sheets, seems to me you owe him for
plagiarizing his life.

ROBBIE

I don't want to hear this again. I think...
(*makes her decision*)
I think I need to do this.

LAURIE

OK. Got it. I can't promise....Don't know if I can do this again.

ROBBIE

You're making me choose. That's pretty dramatic. Blackmail?

LAURIE

No. Not at all. Just telling you my limits. I was patient – even
supportive about New York. We made it through Betsy. All those
late nights. We even made it through the Stan and Sarah siege.
We had practically no time alone. Now you're going to do this
again? To us? To me?

ROBBIE

Think about what happens when I get tenured. We'll have the financial security we really didn't have in New York. It's different this time. And it's more important now because of your loss of income. You could even go back to school and get your DVM.

LAURIE

This isn't about tenure and you know it. It's your mistress, this consuming addiction. Be honest with yourself and with me. It's the third person in bed with us. I can't compete with that.

ROBBIE

You don't have to compete with anything. Tell you what. You just concentrate on getting sober. Everything will look better when you're clean.

LAURIE

Not taking any responsibility for any of this?

ROBBIE

We both have a lot of work to do.

LAURIE

Maybe I need to find someplace else to live for a while.

ROBBIE

No. I don't want you to do that. Please.

LAURIE

I need time to sort all this out. A lot has happened.

ROBBIE

We can't work this out?

LAURIE

I want to. I do. Not sure if we can. I thought Betsy was a threat.
But it's this other passion of yours. Much more intrusive, intense. It won't go away.

ROBBIE

Just give it a little more time. I love you. Please.

Lights Down

SCENE THREE

*Three weeks later. The condo is dark but we can see all traces of
STAN and SARAH have disappeared. A phone is heard ringing in
another part of the house. The first part of the scene is heard offstage.*

LAURIE
(*on phone, groggy*)
Hello? Sarah. Why are you calling so late....Oh, no.

ROBBIE

What? What?

LAURIE
(*on phone*)
What happened?

ROBBIE

What? What's going on?

(lights go on in bedroom area, offstage)

LAURIE

Wait, wait. I'm moving into the living room.

*(In PJs, they both enter the living room, switching on the lights.
ROBBIE is following LAURIE closely)*

ROBBIE
(more insistent)

Laurie! Tell me. What happened?

LAURIE

The club is on fire.
                    (into phone)

Is it bad?

ROBBIE

Is it?

LAURIE
(into phone)

Is anyone hurt?

                    (pause)

Well, that's good. Jeez.

ROBBIE

What happened? How?

LAURIE

It's Sarah.

ROBBIE

Well, I know that much.

LAURIE

(*into phone*)

I'm so sorry.

(*pause*)

Uh huh. That's good.

ROBBIE

What's good?

LAURIE

They're insured. Over-insured, she said.

(*into phone*)

Sarah? Are you OK? You don't sound…all that upset.

ROBBIE

Of course, she's upset. How can she not be upset?

LAURIE

(*into phone*)

Yeah, I know.

ROBBIE

Know what?

LAURIE

(*into phone*)

Please let us know what we can do. Yeah, I understand. It's still terrible that it happened. A total loss? I'm so sorry. Please tell Stan how sorry we are, too. OK. Talk to you later. Thanks. Bye.

(hangs up)

Well.

ROBBIE

(still standing by LAURIE, looking dazed)
How did it happen? What caused it?

LAURIE

They don't know yet. Somebody saw smoke coming out of the
building about 1 a.m. The fire department called Stan. By the
time both of them got there, it was a wall of flames.

ROBBIE

I was just there earlier last night, rehearsing.

LAURIE

Stan said the building was so close to being finished.

ROBBIE

Wonder if the workmen left something on. They were finishing
up when I left. My God.
(she sits, LAURIE joins her on the couch)

LAURIE

What a shock for them.

ROBBIE

For them? Yeah.

LAURIE

Funny, though. I didn't hear any... emotion at all in Sarah's
voice. She sounded like a TV reporter, without much reaction.

ROBBIE

I'm not sure what I'm feeling.

LAURIE

I know you were counting on this.

ROBBIE

Hasn't sunk in.

LAURIE

I wonder if there's anything on the all-night news station yet.
(she goes over to turn on the TV)

TV ANNOUNCER VO

Weather tomorrow will be like today, John, sunny and 73. To follow up on the breaking news, firemen are seen here battling a blaze in a building under construction in West Los Angeles. The fire department arrived around 130 a.m. but the building was completely engulfed. Second alarm was called in a half hour later. The fire's origins have not been determined but one passer-by reported seeing someone speed away in a black van shortly before the fire likely started. Cause of the fire is currently under investigation.

ROBBIE

A black van? Sarah drives a ... Nah. She wouldn't do that. Couldn't have been her.
(she laughs a little).
Sorry. It's not funny. Besides, how would she get away from Stan to torch the place? And why would she do that?

LAURIE

(she laughs a little, too)

We know Stan's a sound sleeper. She did say they were very heavily insured. It was mostly her money that was tied up in there.

ROBBIE

If she did it – and I can't believe that she did – she probably did it for the money.

LAURIE

Or some other reason. A lot going on in there. Issues.

(They sit for a moment, contemplating this possibility)

ROBBIE

Whatever happened, it's all over now.

LAURIE

Stan is totally invested in this. It's his dream. It was all he ever talked about – other than his monstrous talent. He'll rebuild, I'm sure.

ROBBIE

Yeah. Rebuild.

LAURIE

What about you?

ROBBIE

I don't know.
(pause)
These last few weeks of rehearsal... Feeling good about my vocals, the show. It all came back much faster than I had thought.

LAURIE

I haven't asked about it. Didn't want to get the shit stirred up again.

ROBBIE

I know. Haven't said it but I appreciate you hanging in here. I know it wasn't easy for you.
(she reaches for her, massages the back of her neck)

LAURIE

More like resignation.

ROBBIE

I don't want to lose you. Or myself, either. Funny, isn't it. We've both struggled with addiction in a way. Mine doesn't have a rehab program.

LAURIE

Mine hasn't worked all that well, either. Wish my name would move up the list. I think I'm ready this time. Haven't touched a drop in a couple of weeks.

ROBBIE

I've noticed. I think I'm ready, too.

LAURIE

You are? What do you mean?

ROBBIE

Ready to give this up. For good this time.

LAURIE

Stop - performing? Really?

ROBBIE

I know. I'm kind of surprised, too. This week there have just been four or five of us in there, me and the musicians running the show over and over. Singing those great songs. The club's empty, just a few lights on. Last night, standing on the stage with the guys playing behind me, I realized *this* is what I love doing – rehearsing. The feeling of a driving beat behind me, singing inside the music that's playing and engulfing me, living in the moment. It's like we're all breathing at exactly the same time. It's...it's....

LAURIE

Wow. Wish I had something like that.

ROBBIE

All of me fuses together. I'm living the lyric, the music's resonating inside. It's like when I was a kid, imagining what it would be like to be doing this. There's nothing like it. Anywhere. It's hard to talk about. To find the words.

LAURIE

I hear you. Powerful. Wonderful. You're giving me goosebumps. It happened in rehearsal. Doesn't happen when you actually perform?

ROBBIE

An audience can be fun – if they're really with you. But it's almost... a distraction, you know? It removes me, pulls me away from my own experience. It's like the fake DiMaggio signature on the ball. It isn't about me. It's about them. It's not real anymore.

LAURIE

You're just saying this because of the club burning down?

ROBBIE

I've been thinking all this time it was the performing that produced the high. But it's the experience of living on all eight cylinders, right there in rehearsal. I get that in teaching sometimes, too. Less predictably.

LAURIE

I think I understand. Hard to find, huh?

ROBBIE

Yeah. I hadn't been paying attention, I guess. To a lot of things. Looking for that high made me lose sight of ...you for a while.

LAURIE

Yeah, there were times....

ROBBIE

I know. For me, too.

LAURIE

Let me understand. I need to hear this. What about your singing career – and Stan's club?

ROBBIE

Stan has to take care of his own dreams. I'm really done this time.

LAURIE

But that feeling....

ROBBIE

The feeling that's most important to me is the one I have for you. Maybe I'm saving us but really I'm saving me. I don't know what I was thinking, trying to start the career over again. I can sit in at local clubs. Or even have some musicians here for a jam. I know people who would like doing that.

LAURIE

Oh, yeah. I love hearing you sing. Especially like this.

ROBBIE

Thanks.

LAURIE

Well. Out of Stan's disaster has come ... not sure how to phrase it...

ROBBIE

An ending and a beginning, no? I'm so sorry to have put you through this - again.

LAURIE

Yeah. It's OK. Sarah put Stan up to this – getting you involved. That still bothers me. Why would she want to drive us apart?

ROBBIE

I don't know. Maybe it wasn't intentional.

LAURIE

Yeah, maybe. But too close a call for me. Let's go to bed.

(arms around each other, they exit to bedroom)

Lights Down

SCENE FOUR

The condo, a few weeks later. LAURIE, ROBBIE and SARAH are sitting in the living room drinking coffee. There's a celebration balloon hanging upstage, saying "Congratulations."

SARAH

Yay, Robbie, congratulations! Getting tenure on the first try is a big deal, they tell me.

LAURIE

Yeah, it is. We're both very happy – and relieved. You never know how it's gonna go.

SARAH

Can't imagine how you lived with that hanging over your head. You're doing a job you love then – with a single arbitrary decision – someone can decide you can't do it anymore.

LAURIE

Don't have to worry about that now. Woo hoo!

ROBBIE

As I told Laurie, there is just one condition - and this is a bit of a curve ball. They insist the play has to be produced. They want me to direct it, too.

LAURIE

You had those directing classes in college. This has to be easier than writing the thing. Shouldn't be a problem for you.

SARAH

Wonderful! Can hardly wait to see it.

ROBBIE
(obviously uncomfortable)

There's just one thing, one teensy little problem. Not sure how to...um...say this. It's about...

LAURIE

Rob, she knows it's about Stan. I was afraid to tell you.

ROBBIE
(shocked)

You told her!

SARAH

No, she didn't. I found out myself. We were in such close quarters there for a while. Hard to keep any secrets.

ROBBIE

Oh shit. Sarah, I don't know what to say. I hope you don't think.....

SARAH

It's OK. I didn't read it all but what I read made me laugh and – well, it's Stan! No hard feelings at all.

ROBBIE

I'm glad. Can we keep him away from seeing it somehow? I guess we have to tell him it's going to be in town. I don't want him to be hurt. I have to admit, he's kind of grown on me.

SARAH

The funny thing is, he could see it and not even recognize himself. It's the self-protective coating of narcissists, I guess. Anything unflattering has to be about someone else.

ROBBIE

But the obviously boorish behavior. The self-aggrandizement.

SARAH

Not him.

LAURIE

She used actual quotes right out of his mouth.

SARAH

He won't remember any of it. He might even laugh at them. When will the show open?

ROBBIE

I would guess in 6-8 weeks or so. Time for rewrites, pre-production casting – all that stuff. It just has to run for one weekend to meet the requirements.

SARAH

I can hardly wait to see it. I wouldn't worry about Stan. He'll still be in the throes of rebuilding the club. Preoccupied as he is these days. Of course, he's always preoccupied.

LAURIE

I know it's his big dream, but…after he already put in all that work to have it go up in flames. Can't imagine going back and trying again.

SARAH

Yeah, I had hoped he'd get discouraged and move on to other things. He made a mistake with this whole thing. I never should have agreed to it. I wanted him to fail....to not be so damned sure of himself. To feel a sense of humility for once.

(ROBBIE and LAURIE exchange glances)

ROBBIE

Did they ever close the investigation - find out the cause of the fire?

SARAH

No, not yet. Someone probably left a cigarette in one of the banquettes. Could have smoldered for several hours.

ROBBIE

I was there that evening. I don't smoke and neither do the musicians. There were a few workmen there, but...

SARAH
(brushing it off)
It could be that we'll never know. But the insurance company is gonna write us a big fat check. Not much consolation. Sure wish it were going back into savings.

ROBBIE

We have even more good news. Once Laurie is out of rehab, we're getting a cute little pug. We have our name in now.

LAURIE
I'm very excited. We're thinking about calling him DiMaggio.

(knock at the door. Laurie gets up to open the door. It's STAN, who enters)

ROBBIE

How's it going over there?

STAN

A lot of work ahead. I had no idea it would take this much time to repair the damage. And I'm still months away – again. *(notices the balloon)* Oh, yeah. I hear congratulations are in order.

ROBBIE

Yes, they are. Thanks. Yeah.

STAN

So… tenure. What is it you had to do? Give a speech? Write a book?

(all exchange glances)

SARAH

She wrote a play, Stan.

STAN
(perking up, now paying attention)
A play? Really.

SARAH

She teaches theater classes, you know.

STAN

I know, Sarah. I'll bet that was fun to write, huh?

ROBBIE

Wouldn't call it fun, exactly. Never wrote one before.

STAN

Huh. And you teach theater. How'd you get away with that?

SARAH

Stan!

LAURIE

Not everybody has to know how to do everything. Actors don't design the lighting. Costumers don't have to learn how to act.

STAN

I guess so. What's it about?

(another pause, exchanging of looks)

LAURIE

Yes, Robbie, tell Stan what it's about.

SARAH

It's about an egotistical performer who doesn't know how awful he is. And it's hilarious.

STAN

Uh huh. And how is it you know this?

LAURIE

It came up once in conversation, just briefly, a while back.

ROBBIE

It's a comedy and thank God, the committee thought so, too. There are elements in there that could have been seen as uncomfortably dark – for some.

STAN

You know, I knew somebody like that in New York. The guy could only talk about himself. Completely unconcerned with anybody else. He came to my show one night – the Gershwin show, the one that always got standing ovations - and left without saying a word about my performance. Gotta get back on stage as soon as I can. There for a while I wondered what I would do with myself. No gigs, no club. But the phoenix has risen again! Guess you're off the hook for performing for me now, Robbie.

ROBBIE

Yeah. Thanks. It's OK. Fine. Better you than me.

STAN

By the time I'm done rebuilding, I'll be back in fine fettle again.

SARAH

Robbie didn't mention it but part of the tenure agreement is that she has to direct her play at the campus theater in a couple of months. It's going to be presented to the public.

STAN

It's going to be produced? At the university?

ROBBIE

Needs some minor rewrites, then I'll interview production people. I never dreamed it would be produced. Not really. Never even hoped it would be. The hard part's the casting.

(click!)

SARAH

Yeah. Who would want to play such a thick-skinned, unsympathetic character with no talent? How old is he, Robbie?

ROBBIE

In his 50s or so. Some flexibility there. But the lead actor has to have had some theater experience. Good with comedy. Can say outrageous lines with a straight face and make them believable. He's in nearly every scene. It's a tough, demanding role. I'll start the audition process as soon as the rewrites are done.

STAN

You know, Robbie, I am an actor. I was in an off-Broadway play once. It was a comedy, too.

SARAH

Off-off-off Broadway. And you were an emergency fill-in for a friend for one night.

STAN

Everyone said how good I was.

SARAH

Your cousins were all in the front row. They applauded everything you said. Your one line.

STAN

I've done lots of community theater, Sarah, and that's what this is.

SARAH

But what about the club? Who will supervise the work? You don't expect me to do that.

STAN

I can do both. Besides, she wants a professional production. Robbie, you need someone who would throw himself into the part. I want to audition. I think I could play this person.

SARAH
I hate to say this. Talk about ambivalence, but I think he's right.

ROBBIE
Yes, Stan, I think you could. In fact…I'm sure of it.

(all but STAN laugh; he doesn't get it and probably never will)

Curtain

Janet Drake, Private Eye

A dark comedy in one act

The Setting:

Two side-by-side living rooms in two different suburbs of Los Angeles. The one on the left is far more upscale and well-appointed than the one on the right. It is 1984.

The Characters:

SIMON, a middle-aged man, a manager who represents Shelby
SHELBY: an attractive but unpretentious former actress, 45-ish
BERNIE: a man who has represented Carlotta, a slick Hollywood type, about 60
CARLOTTA: a woman past her prime but in denial; thinks she's a grand actress with more than a touch of Norma Desmond; around 60
ARNIE: Slimy schlock producer, can be 40-60
PROCESS SERVER: any age (can also double ARNIE, if necessary)

SCENE ONE

Lights up stage left in SHELBY'S apartment where she is sitting at a desk in her home office, autographing photos. SIMON enters.

SIMON

Hey.

SHELBY

Hey.

SIMON

I love watching you do that.

SHELBY

It's your fault, you know. I wouldn't still be doing this if it weren't for you.

SIMON

The public still loves you.

SHELBY

Well, I don't know about that.

SIMON

Sure they do. You've seen how they crowd around you at those nostalgia shows.

SHELBY

Yeah. I don't understand it, really. Nice, though.

(phone rings; SHELBY answers it)

SHELBY

Hello? Oh, hello, Sue. Yes, he's here. *(hands the phone to SIMON)*
Surprise! It's for you.

SIMON

Hi, hon. We're just going over some plans. Yeah, I did. I said I
had hoped to get home soon, but I just booked another show
for this weekend. *(pause)* I'm sorry. What? Why did you expect
me home for the bridge tournament? Well, I'm sorry, I can't...
wait. I don't play bridge. You must be thinking of some other
husband. No, I'm just kidding. Kidding. Well, I am sorry. I was
sorry yesterday when you called, too. What more can I say? I
know, I know. We'll cross that, uh, bridge when we come to it.
I have to go. Bye. *(he hangs up)* Wish she'd stop calling. I hate
those conversations. No trust. Love her, but...

SHELBY

*(Starts humming the song, "Sweet Sue" singing the words in the
title at the end of the phrase as she dances around the room)*

SIMON

Sweet Sue my ass *(they both laugh)*. She doesn't understand.
Never did. But let's get back to the Daily Variety announcement.

SHELBY

No need.

SIMON

Oh, come on.

SHELBY

That silly detective show was canceled, what, 15 years ago.

SIMON

(theatrically) "Janet Drake, Private Eye. Starring Shelby Clark! The intrepid detective who cleverly solves the crimes that stumped all the experts!" You were marvelous in it.

SHELBY

The sponsors didn't think so.

SIMON

They canceled the series because it was too early. Society wasn't ready for a female hero like Janet Drake. Too much "suspension of disbelief," the critics said. They didn't think women could solve murder cases.

SHELBY

They didn't think women could think. I guess I was lucky we made it through two seasons. Those nostalgia shows, though... well...they're not too bad. The money, either.

SIMON

I know you don't need to do them. You were so smart to have invested your money back then. Most people in the biz have nothing to show for their hard work. Too much carpe diem.

SHELBY

Yeah. Lucky. I love my little beach house nestled here in the canyon.

SIMON

And speaking of luck...

SHELBY

Yes? Planning on going to Vegas?

SIMON

Yeah, the wife would really like that. She's pissed off as it is because of all the time I spend with you.

SHELBY

(sarcastically) She's not jealous. Not really. She's told you that. She knows it's strictly business between us. Right?

SIMON

Most of the time. I mean, most of the time she knows it's business.

SHELBY

I do feel guilty that you sleep on the couch every night. *(her look says she has other desires)*

SIMON

(changing the subject) As I was saying, speaking of luck…

SHELBY

Oh, yeah. What's up?

SIMON

So like I said, there's an article in Daily Variety this morning you will find interesting. It says Arnold Weidler is thinking about making a movie about…

SHELBY

Arnold Weidler? The Sultan of Schlock? Who gets the treatment this time? Not another macho superhero. How is he still in business? Wasn't he under indictment or something for supplying cocaine to some starlet? Please. Ech.

SIMON

Not a superhero. Not really. Not macho, either.

SHELBY

What? *(they exchange looks; she gets it)* No. Janet Drake? *(laughs at the absurdity)*. Oh, come on. He's resurrecting that old broad?

SIMON

It said he was looking around for a writer to polish the script and was starting to think about casting.

SHELBY

Yeah, probably whoever he's screwing this week. Or owes money to.

SIMON

Yeah, maybe. Tell me you aren't interested.

SHELBY

I'm not interested. My world is just fine as it is. See ya later. I'm going to run out and pick up the cleaning. *(she starts to leave)*

SIMON

(stops her) Wait a sec. Shel. Think about this.

SHELBY

Nobody wants to see a middle-aged Janet Drake. With arthritis yet.

SIMON

Did you remember your meds this morning?

SHELBY

Yup. You take good care of me, Simon.

SIMON

Somebody needs to look out for you. Back to Janet Drake.

SHELBY

Audiences want to watch kids. The 20-somethings, not those of us eligible for AARP.

SIMON

It's different now. Look what's on TV. It's Miss Marple on public television.

SHELBY

Oh, thanks. Now I'm a Miss Marple type, huh?

SIMON

No, no. I didn't mean that. OK, then. How about Jessica Fletcher? "Murder She Wrote" made the top ten this season. Angie's no starlet, you know. They probably think it can translate into movies. I'm going to call Weidler. At least we'll know who he's considering.

SHELBY

I don't know.

SIMON

I can't believe I have to talk you into this. What's going on?

SHELBY

I appreciate your enthusiasm, but...

SIMON

But what? It's just a phone call.

SHELBY

This is important to you. Why?

SIMON

OK. You want the truth?

SHELBY

Uh, yeah.

SIMON

I've seen the response at these nostalgia shows. I know you still have juice. And I know you're bored being a ...

SHELBY

Housewife?

SIMON

Sort of. Except you're not a wife. Listen, we can make this happen.

SHELBY

I don't want to be anybody's wife. I've done that before - twice.

SIMON

Three times, if we're counting. Or was it four?

SHELBY

I don't count #2. He wasn't around long enough. Wasn't he the short one? The marriage was. There's still a bullet hole in the wall over there behind the picture. Never did get it fixed.

SIMON

What? What happened?

SHELBY

Yeah. Things got out of hand one night after he threatened to hit me. I pulled out the revolver from the bedroom drawer and almost plugged him. Soooo close.

SIMON

Oh, my God. But you didn't. Why not?

SHELBY

Just wanted to scare him. I didn't think he was worth going to jail over. And this Janet Drake part isn't worth my stressing over, either. No, no. I don't think so.

SIMON

Do you still have the gun?

SHELBY

In the bedroom. You never know these days when you'll need it.

SIMON

Just let me make the call. Don't shoot me down. Shel.

SHELBY

Oh, Simon. I haven't done any real performing in years. I'm too old. Too tired. Too –

SIMON

Scared?

SHELBY

I'm going to go pick up the cleaning. That's something I know how to do. Nobody dies. Nobody gets hurt.

SIMON

You know your problem? You're not narcissistic enough. That's a problem that's in short supply in this business. OK. OK. Truth out. *(he holds up his hands; she stops)* You know I love those autograph shows. But doing them…it's just not enough - for me. The word that comes to mind is trapped.

SHELBY

Is it money you need? You know I'm happy to give you..

SIMON

No, that's not it. I just need more…how can I explain it? Hope, maybe.

SHELBY

Hope? I don't understand. You feel trapped? By me?

SIMON

Yeah. No, it's not you. It's this crazy schedule. I need to be here for those shows, to handle the bookings, the business end, you know. I worry, too. You know that.

SHELBY

You know I appreciate that. But, what - ?

SIMON

I have no life at home with Sue. And no real life anywhere. I feel like a boarder wherever I am. A temp.

SHELBY

Sorry you feel like that. You want me to put myself out there, up there, for you? How will this help your lousy marriage?

SIMON

I don't know that it will. Janet, this is just too good a chance to pass up.

SHELBY

You just called me Janet.

SIMON

See? Even I believe you're that character.

SHELBY

(laughs) Uh huh. Nice move. You forget I'm not the only one who played her.

SIMON

Yeah, I know.

SHELBY

Do you think they'd be interested in her for the role?

SIMON

Nah. She's over the hill.

SHELBY

Well, who isn't? I'm so far over the other side I don't remember the climb. What is she? Fifty? Sixty? Old *(shudders)*.

SIMON

I don't know. Haven't heard anything about her in maybe 20 years. Don't even know if she's still alive.

SHELBY

She's probably fat. Or in a rest home. Or in jail. Or she's had her face lifted so many times she looks like a Pekinese.

SIMON

You didn't have to be beautiful for radio.

SHELBY

I never listened to the show. I was still doing all those low budget movies at Monogram. Of course, I had no idea I'd play Janet on TV. That was sort of a fluke.

SIMON

I wonder if she ever got over that.

SHELBY

Probably not.

SIMON

Do I sense a softening here? Can I make the call?

SHELBY

Oh, sure. *(sarcastically)* What can possibly go wrong?

(SHELBY freezes and SIMON walks downstage and addresses the audience)

SIMON

Let's stop for a minute. You're probably wondering what I'm doing here. Good question. I wish I had a good answer for you. I have a wife who lives 2000 miles away. She drives me crazy. Much of the time I live here with Shelby. Sometimes she drives me crazy, too. Sue is like an air horn, insistent, demanding, difficult. Shelby is like a slow drip, unsettling, but easy. I met Shelby at one of those nostalgia shows. I was running it. I'm a conference organizer by trade, not a manager or agent. We struck up a conversation and hit it off right away. She was married at the time and so was I. Am I. When she asked if I would consider managing her, I didn't know how to respond. I didn't know what a manager did. But I said yes and here I am. All I can do is promote what's left of her career now. She deserves it. I think she deserves better.

SCENE TWO

(Lights have moved stage right, to the small, slightly shabby apartment that belongs to CARLOTTA; she is pacing, clearly agitated when the doorbell rings; she runs to the door, opens it to see BERNIE; throughout the scene she's straightening up the room that doesn't need straightening)

BERNIE
(entering out of breath)
Hi. What's going on? You sounded pretty jazzed on the phone. It's good to see you again, Carlotta. Been a long time. What's with the three-story walkup? I thought those were only in New York.

CARLOTTA
Sorry. The elevator is always on the fritz.

BERNIE
I gotta sit for a minute and catch my breath. Three flights ain't easy.

CARLOTTA

Bernie. Did you see Daily Variety this morning?

BERNIE

Well, sure. Over coffee, every morning. I see Brown and Zanuck are going to do a picture with a bunch of geezers. Called
"Cocoon." I'm going to try to get Wilfred Brimley in that. He
hasn't done much in...

CARLOTTA

Forget that. I'm talking about Arnold Weidler, not some geezer.

BERNIE

OK. You know, Carlie, Baby, you don't look half bad. How
long has it been? Three-four years? Um, maybe a little longer.

CARLOTTA

I didn't call you over for a chorus of "Auld Lang Syne." And
damned right I look good.

BERNIE

Yeah, yeah. Good. So what's up?

CARLOTTA

You'll never believe this. Weidler is going to do a remake of
"Janet Drake, Private Eye."

BERNIE

Oh, yeah. Saw that. Didn't you do that on the radio like thirty,
forty years ago?

CARLOTTA

Absolutely not! Yes, I did create the character and starred on
the radio. It definitely was not thirty years ago. It was only...

mmmm…less than twenty. That's my role. I created her out of thin air. I am Janet Drake.

BERNIE

Yeah, I didn't represent you then. Wasn't that also on TV?

CARLOTTA

That woman stole it from me. She's a Drake impersonator.

BERNIE

Boy, that was a long time ago, sweetie.

CARLOTTA

I want Janet Drake back. She's mine. I should have sued her for theft. Or slander. Or something. I never watched it, of course. None of those 52 episodes. I'm sure she was awful. Terrible overacting. Especially the one where she was kidnapped and—

(sudden loud banging next door)

BERNIE

What the hell is that?

CARLOTTA

The people next door were evicted last week. Not happy about it, either. I don't know what's going on over there. Not my business. All kinds of crazy things go on over there.

BERNIE

Are you telling me you want this part? Is that what you're saying?

CARLOTTA

I have always been Janet Drake. It was created for me. Bernie, you're my agent. You can get this for me.

BERNIE

Well, I…uh…

CARLOTTA

You owe me this. I've paid out a lot in commissions over the past..um…many years. And all you've gotten me are those crappy little cameos in sci-fi films. I couldn't go on playing the creature's earth mother forever.

BERNIE

You turned down the last part I got for you. It wasn't easy to convince the producer you were right for the little werewolf's babysitter.

CARLOTTA

I know. I just couldn't…But now, this is the real thing. I could get back to where I belong.
            (starts to cough and gag)

BERNIE

What's wrong? Need water?

CARLOTTA

I think I just swallowed a fly. Water!
            (he gets some from the other room; she drinks)
I gotta get those screens fixed.

BERNIE

Look, babe.

CARLOTTA

Don't "look, babe" me. You just do your goddamned job.

BERNIE

You don't remember firing me?

CARLOTTA

I never fired you. Well. That was a mistake. I want you back. I want it all back. You want a drink? Got some vodka. Or rum.

BERNIE

Not before lunch. So hot in here.

CARLOTTA

The AC went out a week or so ago.

BERNIE

I don't know how you stand it. Humid, too.

CARLOTTA
(sidles up to BERNIE)
I'd do anything to get this part.

BERNIE

(moving away) Yeah, I remember the "anything" from before.

CARLOTTA

You know I can do it. I know I can do it.

BERNIE

Listen, Toots. How about I talk to someone at Fox. I think there's a big swimming pool scene in that "Cocoon" movie. Maybe I can get you a bit over there. They'll need lots of background people. Maybe even a line or two. Hey, it's with Don Ameche. Remember him?

CARLOTTA

You're not getting this, Bernie. I am not a background player. I am a star. I was the star of that damned radio show. Our Hooper ratings were above all the rest. Everyone wanted to work with me. I loved being loved.

BERNIE

(carefully) Lemme ask ya. Why do you think you didn't get the TV show?

CARLOTTA

If I'd had a good agent like you, I would have.

BERNIE

Yeah. You would have been a shoe-in, seems to me. Didn't ya audition? You done the radio show and...

CARLOTTA

Did you ever meet Roger Gormley? That old coot.

BERNIE

Head of the network.

CARLOTTA

I did everything I could to show him I should be the one to do it. Everything.

BERNIE

Ah, yeah. The anything, everything...

CARLOTTA

Didn't even get an audition. He said I was too old. After we...met.

BERNIE

Ouch.

CARLOTTA

He's wrong. I wasn't. And I'm not now, either. I'm still in my prime.

BERNIE

Uh huh. What happened to, what's her name, Shelby Clark? Didn't she end up playing Janet Drake?

CARLOTTA

I have no idea where she is. Or care. I'm sure she's old and fat. Maybe in jail. After all, she stole that part from me. Or maybe she's in a rest home. Poor thing. She's probably had her face lifted so many times she looks like Howdy Doody.

BERNIE

All women in Hollywood get done. It's no crime.

CARLOTTA

Look at this face. I have never, ever had plastic surgery.

BERNIE

(laughs) Mmm hmmm. Have you met her? You know her?

CARLOTTA

No. And I have no interest in doing that, either. Lousy thief.

BERNIE

Aw, come on, sweetheart. Let it go.

CARLOTTA

Can't you just get me a chance to read?

BERNIE

You'd get trampled in a cattle call. You ready for that?

CARLOTTA

The cream always rises to the top.

BERNIE

And it curdles when it's left out too long. I don't even know what they're looking for.

CARLOTTA

They're looking for me.

BERNIE

(wearing down) OK, OK, I'll check into it.

CARLOTTA

I'll even increase your percentage to 15%.

BERNIE

That's what it's been for a long time, Carlie.

CARLOTTA

(facing him, intensely)

Repeat after me. I will get this for you, Carlotta.

BERNIE

I can't promise, doll. I can't. You know that.

CARLOTTA
(pounds on the couch)
Say it. Say it. Say it.

BERNIE
I'll try. That's all I can do.

CARLOTTA
You owe me, Bernie. Say it.

BERNIE
(shakes his head) I'll do my best. *(puts his arms around her)*

CARLOTTA
I know you will. How about we relax a little in the other room?
A little massage, maybe. *(she tries to coax him into the bedroom)*
I remember how to relax you.

BERNIE
I don't have much time. I have a meeting in a half hour.

CARLOTTA
You'll make it. As I remember, it won't take long.
*(they start to exit but BERNIE stops, returns to downstage and
addresses the audience)*

BERNIE
Hey, what was I gonna do? She's like all the others. She wants
to be a star. Of course, she thinks she **is** a star. She hasn't been
my most successful client, not by a long shot. The business
has changed since radio. How can I tell her that? She looks
in the mirror and sees the 20-something woman who could

turn heads. I didn't mind getting her small parts over the years. She needed to live, just like the rest of us. Looks to me like she never saved a penny of it. She needs a job. But I'm not the hustler I was years ago, either. Everything changes. I kind of feel sorry for her. Besides, she's a client with benefits. It's not like it's personal. This could get me back in the game. She's a pain in the ass but you never want to say never. Anybody can score big in Hollywood—if you're the one they're looking for.

SCENE THREE

(SHELBY's house a few days later, SIMON is on the phone)

SIMON
How many actors are you looking at?

SHELBY
Probably too many.

SIMON
That's it?

SHELBY
I hate competition. Acting shouldn't be a competitive sport.

SIMON
I'd like to bring Shelby Clark in next Friday at 3. Can we do that?

SHELBY

Why?

SIMON

OK. Thanks. Yeah, I'll bring in a current photo.

SHELBY

I don't have one. Unless you count the picture my sister took at the New Year's Eve party. Not my best angle. And I was pretty wasted by then.

SIMON

Thanks very much, Rich. I owe you one.
(hangs up)

SHELBY

Tell me again - why am I doing this.

SIMON

(takes a long look at her)
Be honest. Don't you miss it?

SHELBY

What? The getting up at 5, the grueling days on the set, the mindless interviews, fending off the men, being cheerful all day, coming home being too tired to eat? Oh, yeah.

(phone rings)

SIMON

Maybe he forgot something. I'll get it. Hey, Rich, whatcha got? Oh, hi, Sue.

(SHELBY leaves the room)

Oh, no, no. Not a problem. Shelby and I were setting up an audition. Very exciting and…No, not that. Of course, I answered the phone because…Why does your sick little mind always go there? What do you want? I told you we have a show every weekend this month. I can't come back now. I'm sorry but I'm trying to earn a living here. She is not. No. This is dumb. I'm hanging up. *(he does)*

SHELBY
(returns to the room)
Again? What does she want now?

SIMON
Same as usual. Wants me home. I hate it when she insults you. Hey, they're sending over your sides for the audition this afternoon.

SHELBY
OK. I guess it doesn't hurt to read.

SIMON
One more thing. They are also considering Carlotta and a few others.

SHELBY
(laughs) So she's still alive, huh? Wonder what she's been doing all these years. And I thought I was over the hill. I'll do this, Si, but my heart's not in it. I'll need your help. Carlotta, huh?

SIMON
You're a pro. It won't take you long to get back into character. I guess I should tell you. I confess I never really watched the show.

SHELBY

That's OK. I didn't, either. *(they both laugh)*. The days were so long. You know, we did it all on film back then. No videotape. Hot lights. Got home late and had to memorize pages. Hope it's different now.

SIMON

You're sounding like you know you'll get it.

SHELBY

Well *(a little embarrassed)*. Yeah, I guess so. I never wanted to be a big star. Still don't. I just wanted to work.

SIMON

And work you will. "The Return of Janet Drake starring Shelby Clark coming to a theater near you!"

(SIMON steps downstage and addresses the audience)

I know she'll get this part, but producers can tell when an actor isn't committed. Maybe I need this more than she does. She'll go along with it. Once she gets a taste of all that again.

SCENE FOUR

(CARLOTTA's apartment. She's lying on the couch, fanning herself to stay cool, thumbing through a magazine; knock at the door – it's BERNIE)

CARLOTTA
(fanning herself)
Hiya. So hot. I'm dying in here.

BERNIE

Wait 'til you hear my news. You got an audition!

CARLOTTA
(throws her arms around him)

Oh, Bernie. You're wonderful!

BERNIE

Yeah, I know. Weidler's AD and I go back a long ways. It's two weeks from Friday in Weidler's office.

CARLOTTA

What about a script?

BERNIE

It's coming over today. And, um…

CARLOTTA

This can't get any better. I'm poised on the threshold of my great return!

BERNIE

Gotta tell ya, sweetie. There'll be other people at the audition.

CARLOTTA

Sure, sure. But they're calling me in. They know I'm the original Janet Drake. The one and only. The others would be pale imitations. They're just going through the motions. Wonder what I should wear. Whaddaya think? Upscale casual? Maybe a long scarf. Or a business suit. Gotta look professional, ya know, like Janet Drake.

BERNIE

One of the actresses is Shelby Clark.

CARLOTTA

Still around, huh? I'm not afraid of her. Anybody can do TV. Radio took talent. It took real skill when all I had was my voice. No fancy camera angles, no fade in fade out. People don't have to use their imagination anymore. It's all handed to them, gimmicks, special effects. All we had was our script and a sound man. We created a world of intrigue and mystery. Janet Drake, Private Eye! Great years.

BERNIE

Great part.

CARLOTTA

Bernie, I need you.

BERNIE

Hey, you got the audition. It's up to you now.

CARLOTTA

Yeah. When I didn't get the TV show, well, things weren't easy.

BERNIE

Well, remember, I didn't know you then.

CARLOTTA

Those next few years were...let's just say Janet Drake was far behind me. When I contacted you a few years later, I had pulled myself back together, ready to try again.

BERNIE

I got you parts. They weren't very big. It was all I could do.

CARLOTTA

Enough to keep me afloat. The last couple of years, though.
Nothing. Been living on alimony checks. All those husbands
were good for something.

BERNIE

Sorry. It's a tough business. Everybody gets hurt. Most dreams
don't come true. I learned that a long time ago.

CARLOTTA

If this comes though, Bern, I'll be back on top. I really need
this. I don't have much time left.

BERNIE

Huh? You dyin' on me?

CARLOTTA

Nah, nothing like that. My landlord is getting testy about the
back rent. I don't have much time to get it to her.

BERNIE

I didn't know you were this…

CARLOTTA

Yeah. Yeah.

BERNIE

I can front you a little…

CARLOTTA

It's gonna be OK. This part is mine. It's always been mine. The
real Janet Drake is back!

BERNIE

Let's not get our hopes up, doll. Hey, we'd all like to be Cinderella. It doesn't happen very often.

CARLOTTA

Bette Davis did it. Joan Crawford did it. Well, almost. If they can do it...

BERNIE

This ain't Warner Bros. Weidler probably has a furnished rented office downtown somewhere.

CARLOTTA

I don't care. I just want another shot. It's all I've ever wanted.

BERNIE

You're kind of feisty, ya know.

CARLOTTA

I can do one of the scenes from the old radio show.
(she's recounting the scene, all done without much acting
and no physical motion)
I was backed up against the wall. The gangsters were both holding guns, ready to shoot. But I stiffened my spine.
"Go ahead and shoot, boys. The police will be here any minute."
And when they got closer, I reached out and grabbed one of the guns. "Take that, you thug." And just then the police came in. The cop said, "Janet Drake, you did it again." I was marvelous.

BERNIE

(steps downstage and addresses the audience)
I think you can tell. She wasn't all that great an actress. And these days the business is moving so fast. It's use it or lose it.

She thinks I'm still the best agent in town. Wish that was true. But maybe Weidler will see how much she wants this. After all, she's well known for "doing anything" to get the part.

SCENE FIVE

Waiting room, Arnold Weidler's rented office; stark setting with folding chairs, coffee table with statue on it it's two weeks later (SIMON and SHELBY enter and see BERNIE there, alone)

SHELBY

Bernie! What are you doing here? Haven't seen you in...years. You're looking good.

BERNIE

Uh, hi, Shelby. How ya doin'?

SHELBY

Why are you here? What a surprise. Are you representing someone in this fight?

SIMON

How do you guys know each other?
                    (turns to BERNIE).
Hi. I'm Simon Flynn.

BERNIE
(they shake hands)

Bernie Goldman.

SHELBY

(to BERNIE) So? What's–? *(to SIMON)* Bernie represented me in the negotiations for the TV series. He's really the reason I was paid so well. Wish it could have gone on longer. You left me.

SIMON

(laughs) You represented Shelby?

BERNIE

(embarrassed). Yeah. Uh, please don't mention it to Carlotta.

SHELBY

So you've moved down the food chain, huh? Charity work, helping the unfortunate. The undertalented. How sweet.

(SHELBY sees a heavy statue on the table, picks it up and examines it)

BERNIE

Lay off, Shel. The kid could use a break.

SHELBY

And where is our elderly diva?

BERNIE

I think she's throwing up in the bathroom.

SIMON

I'm surprised she's so nervous.

BERNIE

I don't think it's nerves. It was the process server at the door this morning. Damned landlord. He couldn't even wait a few more weeks.

SHELBY

She's being evicted? Oh, my God. That's awful *(stifling a laugh)*.

BERNIE

Yeah. She really needs this part. Arnie told me it's down to just the two of you and I know she's hoping…

SIMON

None of my business but how did it come to this?

BERNIE

I don't know. You know, she'd be pissed if she knew I was talking about her.

SHELBY

I don't know what to say. So if I get it, I'm the bad guy, huh? Ripping the food right out of her busy mouth.

SIMON

No, Shel. Not your responsibility to take care of her.

SHELBY

Yeah. Bernie, can't you do something. That doesn't involve me?

BERNIE

It wasn't easy getting her this audition.

SIMON

But she was the original Janet Drake.

(SIMON and SHELBY exchange looks)

BERNIE

But not well remembered, if you know what I mean. She was knockin' 'em back pretty good then and was canned. Sorta hush-hush. I heard that from a friend who worked on the show. That's why it was so easy for you to be cast in the TV version.

SHELBY

Easy? I don't think so. I saw an interview she gave when that happened. She trashed me pretty good. I never understood why she was so—

(CARLOTTA enters the room, a little the worse for wear)

CARLOTTA

Is it time?

BERNIE

You have a few minutes. Carlie, this is Shelby Clark, Simon Flynn. Carlotta Van Sandt.
(they shake hands and all sit in silence; SHELBY and CARLOTTA sneak peeks at each other; CARLOTTA tries to straighten things around her)

SHELBY

So, Carlotta. How have things been going for you?

CARLOTTA

Oh. Wonderful. I had four auditions last week alone. I was telling Bernie I don't know if I have time to do this film. So nice to be in demand. *(to SHELBY)* Hey, you don't look so bad...for your age.

(SHELBY picks up the statue again, slapping it on its side)

(MAN enters, looks around, is carrying legal papers;
sees CARLOTTA)

MAN

Oh, hello, Miss Van Sandt. Nice to see you again.

CARLOTTA

Uh. What are you doing here? Now what?

BERNIE

Who's this guy?

MAN

I'm the one who delivered her eviction notice this morning.
Thanks for asking me in. Sorry I couldn't stay long.

(SHELBY and SIMON turn away, laughing;
MAN looks at BERNIE)

Are you Simon Flynn?

BERNIE

That's him.

SIMON

That's me.

MAN
(handing him a legal paper)
Consider yourself served.

SHELBY

What? What's this about? How did you find him?

(SIMON reads the papers)

MAN

I followed you. Not easy this job. Lemme tell ya. They don't pay me enough.

SIMON

She's suing me for divorce. Alienation of affection. It says co-respondent: Shelby Clark.

SHELBY

Me? Wow. I wish.

CARLOTTA

What does that mean?

BERNIE

His wife knows he's screwing Shelby and wants out.

SHELBY

That's not true. I am not. Stop saying that. Simon, how can this happen?

MAN

Now I'm looking for a Bernie Goldman.

(BERNIE backs into the corner)

SHELBY

Ha. That's him. Right there. The cowering little man in the corner.

(MAN hands him a legal paper)

What is this? Discount day at the courthouse? *(turns to MAN)*
Big day for you, huh? Your mother must be very proud.

CARLOTTA

Bernie?

BERNIE

It's an old client. Suing me. No grounds. No reason at all. Nothing
new. I can make it go away. Happens all the time. Cranks.

SHELBY

Gee, I'm feeling left out here. No papers for me?

SIMON

Isn't it enough to be named in the divorce action?

CARLOTTA

Disappointed it's not the starring role, dear?

SHELBY

At least, I have a place to sleep tonight.

CARLOTTA

And a bed partner, too.

*(as SHELBY picks up the statue menacingly, we hear a voice at
the door to the office; all freeze)*

ARNOLD (v.o.)

Janet Drake?

(CARLOTTA AND SHELBY both eagerly rise and move toward the door)

CARLOTTA and SHELBY

Yes!

ARNOLD (v.o.)

Oh, I'm sorry. I meant Miss Clark. Miss Clark? Would you come in, please? Hi. I'm Arnold Weidler. Arnie.

(SHELBY puts the statue down, smiles at CARLOTTA and enters the inner office)

SIMON

It's always good to be seen first. Sets the standard.

CARLOTTA

Yeah. Low.

BERNIE

Hey, come over here and sit. Take a few minutes before he calls you in. Everything's gonna be fine. You'll see. Carlotta, look at me: You are Janet Drake!

(CARLOTTA ignores him, sits, holds her head in her hands, pushes imaginary dust off the table while BERNIE and SIMON read their legal documents)

SCENE SIX

*Still in casting offices but CARLOTTA is not there; BERNIE on
one side of the room, the other two on the opposite side*

BERNIE

Hey, Simon. Can I see you for a sec?

SIMON

OK.
(moves to be next to him)
What's up, buddy?

BERNIE

Um. Um. You know, I've gone to a lot of trouble to get this
audition for Carlotta.

SIMON

Uh huh. It was trouble? I'll bet.

BERNIE

Well. Not really. Um.

SIMON

What's your point?

BERNIE

Carlie needs this. You know, she—

SIMON

Yeah, well, every actress wants the part. That's what Hollywood's
all about.

BERNIE

Yeah, yeah. I know.

SIMON

I'm not so sure Shelby wants it, to be honest.

BERNIE

What do you mean she doesn't want it?

SIMON

She does, but…I had to talk her into this audition.

BERNIE

Aw, come on.

SIMON

We do these nostalgia shows, you know. She's very big there.

BERNIE

Yeah. I tried to get Carlie into those, but nobody knows radio stars no more.

SIMON

Shelby had a long movie career. Not a star, of course. But a ton of Bs.

BERNIE

I know, I know. But I thought once an actress, always an actress.

SIMON

You'd think. But she's happy with those shows. She likes them. It's enough.

BERNIE

Listen. What do I have to do to get you guys to…step aside here?

SIMON

She'd never do that.

BERNIE

Everybody has a price.

SIMON

What's the matter with you? You don't think Carlotta can get this part on her own?

BERNIE

She needs this. OK, I need this, too.

SIMON

Hey, I'm sorry. But I can't help you, man. You shouldn't even be asking. Back off.

BERNIE

I gotta get it for her. I been working on this for a while. I know Carlie would do anything for this. I'm counting on that. Arnold is, too. I've done…some…things…I wouldn't normally–

SIMON

I don't want to hear this. Look, I'm sorry. But you know how this works. It's about talent.

BERNIE

You're a dreamer. That isn't always what gets the job.

SIMON

Whatever you had to do, I hope it was worth it to you. Because the job is Shelby's.

(both men stand and move toward each other, menacingly; BERNIE shoves SIMON; SHELBY moves to separate them)

SHELBY

Hey, come on, you guys. Stop this. Stop. What's going on? Simon?

SIMON

Come on, Bernie. Tell Shelby what we were talking about. *(to SHELBY)* He was trying to talk me into taking you and walking out.

SHELBY

What? Why?

BERNIE

Nah. Just trying to do a deal. That's all.

SIMON

Tell Shelby what you did to get Carlotta this audition.

(CARLOTTA returns, all smiles)

CARLOTTA

(to BERNIE) I was wonderful. You should have seen it. Like old times. I got inside Janet Drake's character and–

ARNIE (v.o.)

Miss Clark? Can I see you again for a minute?

(she exits, looking behind her)

CARLOTTA

I'm sure I got this. He loved me.

BERNIE

Of course, you do, Sweetie. In the bag. I told you.

SIMON

So, Carlotta.

BERNIE

Don't start with her.

CARLOTTA
(to SIMON)

What?

BERNIE

I'm warning you.

SIMON

Just a few questions.

BERNIE

Don't do it.

CARLOTTA
(to SIMON)

Shoot.

SIMON

Bernie boy, here, thinks you're pretty hot...to get this part.

BERNIE

Knock it off.

SIMON

In fact, he thinks you'll do anything to get it. Like he did.

CARLOTTA
(to BERNIE)
What's he talking about? *(to SIMON)* And I would not. Do
anything. What did you - ?

SIMON

Isn't that what you said, Bernie? That both of you would do
anything..Just a couple of—

BERNIE
(moves aggressively toward SIMON, they start to scuffle)

CARLOTTA
(stands back and watches)
Hey, I haven't had two men fight over me since…well, in a long
time. Don't hurt each other, boys. Hit him, Bern.

(eventually they stop when SIMON is knocked to the floor)

(SHELBY enters to see what's going on)

SHELBY

We heard the noise out here. Arnie is calling Security.

SIMON
(straightens himself up)

That won't be necessary. I've said what I wanted to say.

BERNIE

I toldja. You better knock it off…I got a lot more for you if you want it.

SIMON

(to SHELBY)

I'm OK. You can go back in there now. Sorry to interrupt the audition.

SHELBY

Well, I'm done.

BERNIE

He dumped you right away, huh? Hard to hear bad news, ain't it?

(SIMON advances on BERNIE)

SHELBY

I'm sorry, Simon. I just can't do it.

CARLOTTA

(in disbelief) He wants to sleep with you, too?

SHELBY

No, Carlotta.

SIMON

You shouldn't have to put out to get a job – unlike some others I could mention.

SHELBY

Si, I told you. Maybe I should have been more explicit. This is my fault. I know how much you want this for me. Well, for you.

SIMON

It's not about me.

CARLOTTA

No, it's about me. You're out of this? Then I got the part!

BERNIE

What just happened here?

SHELBY
(to SIMON)

Just coming here today. Brought it all back. The meat on the hoof. The competition.

BERNIE

If you can't take the heat, Girlie, you don't belong in this business.

SIMON
(to BERNIE)

Just shut up.

SHELBY

He's right. I don't. I don't want to be Janet Drake. I just want to be Shelby Clark. Look, I like being a has-been. I can sit at my desk and autograph photos for fans who don't annoy me when I go to the market. I can go to those autograph shows and get paid pretty well for just a few hours of creating some good memories for people. Then I can go home.

No scripts, no hours in makeup, no lines to memorize, no stupid interviews, no casting couches. No pretending to be somebody I'm not.

SIMON

No chance to be a big movie star.

CARLOTTA

What's the matter with you?

BERNIE

She's crazy, Sweetie. She don't know what's good.

SHELBY

That's where you're wrong, Bernie. I do. And this isn't it. Come on, Simon. Let's go home.

(SHELBY and SIMON exit as ARNIE enters; BERNIE leaps up and shakes his hand)

BERNIE

Hey, Arnie. Good to see you again. You know what happened, right? Shelby walked out.

ARNIE

Yeah. I understand. I made a few quick phone calls. Things have changed.

CARLOTTA

And now there's nothing standing in the way of my being…my returning as Janet Drake, Private Eye!

BERNIE

We can do the deal today. Get things rolling. She can go over to wardrobe right away.

ARNIE

Sugar, why do you want to do this? It's been a long time since you've been Janet Drake. Since you've done much of anything in the business. I don't think you want to put yourself through this, honey. It wouldn't be easy for someone of...your age.

CARLOTTA

I can play any age. Ask Bernie. Just give me a chance to prove it. Tell him, Bernie.

BERNIE

Ya want a younger Janet Drake? We can get her a facelift. Just a couple of weeks off. She had one ten years ago or so, didn't ya, honey?

CARLOTTA
(not happy to hear this)

Uh. Maybe.

ARNIE

I'm bringing in some big names to read. Younger. You know. I'm sorry, Bernie. I can't help you.

BERNIE

But Arnie, you promised.

ARNIE

Well, that wasn't exactly what we agreed to the other night. I tell ya what. There's a small part in one scene for Janet's mother. It's not much but all attention would be on you.

CARLOTTA

(*shocked*) The mother? An old lady? You want me to play a—

BERNIE

Carlie, it might not be so bad. You're an actress, remember.

CARLOTTA

Not bad? But Janet Drake is an adult, middle-aged. Me, play Janet Drake's mother?

ARNIE

Otherwise...

BERNIE

She'll do it.

CARLOTTA

(*deep sigh*) I'll do it.

ARNIE

OK. Good. While we're doing the deal, why don't the two of you come into my office, get comfortable. We can discuss, you know, what we might be able to do for each other. I have an hour before my next appointment (*CARLOTTA smiles, BERNIE not so much*).

(*CARLOTTA and BERNIE exit into ARNIE'S office*)

End of Play

CLOSING CREDITS

Acknowledgements

Though the magic of Hollywood has always flowed through my veins, my introduction to writing fiction is relatively recent. For this abrupt U-turn into the unknown, I thank Tod Goldberg, who directs the Low Residency MFA program in Creative Writing and Writing for the Performing Arts at the University of California, Riverside. Tod convinced me that it was possible that this stubborn connoisseur of nonfiction might be harboring a latent imagination. Due to his encouragement and gentle handholding, I tip-toed into this strange land. I admit I cheated a little and framed the stories around my affinity with Hollywood's history. Thanks also to Mickey Birnbaum, another UCR faculty member, who shoved me off the creative cliff into the murky waters of playwriting.

Others who offered essential and appreciated constructive criticism are Cheryl Castles (stories and plays), teacher Mary Otis (stories) and dramaturg Michael Kinghorn (plays). A special thanks to Artistic Director Gina Bikales for selecting the two plays in this book that opened separate staged reading seasons for Script2Stage2Screen in Rancho Mirage, CA. A big thanks goes to Shanna McNair and Scott Wolven of The Writer's Hotel in New York for their thoughtful consideration of the entire manuscript. Deservedly warm regards go to Larry Ward for his years of support and friendship, one that unsurprisingly started with a Hollywood connection.

And finally, much literary affection goes to Stevan V. Nikolic, the founding editor and publisher of Adelaide Books and Adelaide Literary Magazine, who has expressed seemingly unconditional confidence in me, whether I submitted nonfiction essays, short stories, plays, or even a book or two.

To everyone who aided and abetted this project, my humble gratitude.

Previous Publications

"Frances"
Scarlet Leaf, January 15, 2018
Fiction on the Web, October 1, 2018

"Dinner with Daddy" published as "Phantom at the Table"
Literary Earth, Spring, 2018
Furtive Dalliance, Summer, 2018
Scarlet Leaf, November, 2018

"Delayed Flight"
TreeHouse Arts, September, 2017

"The Last Fan"
Escapism, Summer, 2017

"Deconstructing Doris"
Writing in a Woman's Voice, September 20, 2017

"The Curtain Never Falls"
Bangladesh Review, 2019

"Madelyn, Mostly"
TreeHouse Arts, February 3, 2017
Short-list winner in *Adelaide Best of 2018*

"Ethel"
Literary Yard, August 4, 2019

"Everything That Mattered"
Adelaide Best of 2019

"Gerry's Interview"
Blue Lake Review, March 1, 2020

Productions and Awards

"Life Without"

Finalist, Ebell Women's Playwriting Competition, 2016
Script2Stage2Screen (Rancho Mirage, CA) opening
production, 2016
Nominated by Desert Theatre League for Outstanding
Production, Bill Groves Award for Original Writing,
Outstanding Comedic Actor, Outstanding Direction
(Arnie Kleban, winner, Outstanding Comedic Actor)

"Janet Drake, Private Eye"

One of four plays in "That Screwy, Ballyhooey Hollywood:
Four Dark Comedies Starring Women of a Certain Age"
Script2Stage2Screen (Rancho Mirage, CA) opening
production, 2018
Finalist, Ruckus Rockwell (Los Angeles, CA), 2018
Alternate, William Inge Festival, 2018

Notes on Songs and Lyrics Mentioned in "Madelyn, Mostly"

My schemes are just like all my dreams,
Ending in the sky
(from "I'm Always Chasing Rainbows," by Harry Carroll and
Joseph McCarthy, 1917)
Public domain

All your fears are foolish fancies, maybe
(from "My Melancholy Baby," by Ernie Burnett and George
A. Norton, 1912)
Public domain

Music is a language lovers understand
Melody and romance wander hand in hand
(from "Say It with Music," by Irving Berlin, 1921)
Public domain

Hello, Dolly.
Well, Hello, Dolly
(from "Hello, Dolly," by Jerry Herman, 1964)
Fair use

Won't someone hear my plea
And take a chance with me
(from "Nobody's Baby," by Milton Ager, Benny Davis, and
Lester Santly, 1921)
Public domain

They go wild, simply wild over me
They go mad, just as made as they can be
(from "They Go Wild Simply Wild Over Me," by Fred Fisher
and Joseph McCarthy, 1917)
Public domain

Now, dearie, don't be late
I want to be there when the band starts playin.'
(from "Darktown Strutters' Ball by Shelton Brooks, 1917)
Public domain

Come Fly with Me
(by Jimmy Van Heusen and Sammy Cahn, 1957)
Fair use

Someone to Watch Over Me
(by George and Ira Gershwin, 1926)
Fair use

Books by Pam Munter

Almost Famous: A Life in and Out of Show Biz

When Teens Were Keen: Freddie Stewart and
the Teen Agers of Monogram

As Alone As I Want To Be

Fading Fame: Women of a Certain Age in Hollywood

About the Author

Pam Munter has authored several books including *When Teens Were Keen: Freddie Stewart and The Teen Agers of Monogram* (Nicholas Lawrence Press, 2005) and *Almost Famous: In and Out of Show Biz* (Westgate Press, 1986) and is a contributor to many others. She's a retired clinical psychologist, former performer and film historian. Her many lengthy retrospectives on the lives of often-forgotten Hollywood performers and others have appeared in *Classic Images* and *Films of the Golden Age*. More recently, her essays and short stories have more than 150 publications. She is the nonfiction book reviewer for *Fourth and Sycamore*. Her play Life Without was a semi-finalist in the Ebell of Los Angeles Playwriting Competition and was nominated for the Bill Groves Award for Outstanding Original Writing, along with a nomination for Outstanding Play in the Staged Reading category. Her second play, *That Screwy, Ballyhooey Hollywood*, will open the new season for Script2Stage2Screen in Rancho Mirage, CA. She has an MFA in Creative Writing and Writing for the Performing Arts. Her memoir, *As Alone As I Want To Be,* was published by Adelaide Books in October 2018. You can find much of her writing at www.pammunter.com.

Made in the USA
Middletown, DE
18 April 2021